'Merry Chris [...] *said softly.*

The room was alig[...] every surface—re[...] large. The flames filled the room with a pale yellow glow that illuminated the small tree decorated in the corner, with presents of various sizes piled up beneath it. On the wall, he'd hung a stocking with her name written in gold.

'I thought you should have a real Christmas,' he said. 'It was the one thing I could think of to pay you back.'

She turned, and her face was shining, brilliant with light that burst from within her. And there were tears streaming down her face. 'Zane,' she said, and her voice broke. She simply moved across the room and flung herself into his arms, gripping him so tightly he could barely breathe.

Finally, all the waiting was over.

Zane kissed her.

And this time, he held nothing back.

Dear Reader,

Welcome. We've some wonderful Christmas treats for you in Sensation™ this month, so you can take a little time and indulge yourself—*whenever* you get the opportunity!

Suzanne Brockmann's visiting with another TALL, DARK AND DANGEROUS man in *It Came Upon a Midnight Clear*—I wouldn't mind waking up and finding Crash Hawken under *my* Christmas tree!

Then there's everybody's favourite, Linda Turner, with *Christmas Lone-Star Style*, another story set in the old house in San Antonio where you ENTER SINGLE, and LEAVE WED…

Then historical author Patricia Potter makes a terrific debut with *Home for Christmas*, where our hero's a cop wrongly convicted. It is easy to see why Patricia's had books on the *USA Today* bestseller list!

Finally, award-winning writer Ruth Wind sends a secret agent to visit an ordinary B&B, and when the bullets start to fly, he's suddenly on the run with the pretty landlady. That's *For Christmas, Forever*—it's certainly not your average Christmas.

Don't miss one of them!

The Editor

For Christmas, Forever

RUTH WIND

SILHOUETTE
SENSATION

*First published in Great Britain 1999
Silhouette Books, Eton House, 18-24 Paradise Road,
Richmond, Surrey TW9 1SR*

© Barbara Samuel 1998

ISBN 0 373 07898 6

18-9912

*Printed and bound in Spain
by Litografia Rosés S.A., Barcelona*

RUTH WIND

is an award-winning author of both contemporary and historical romances. She lives in the mountainous South West U.S.A with her husband, two growing sons and many animals in a hundred-year-old house the town blacksmith built. The only hobby she has since she started writing is tending the ancient garden of irises, lilies and lavender beyond her office window, and she says she can think of no more satisfying way to spend a life than growing children, books and flowers.

For Teresa Hill, a.k.a. Sally Tyler Hayes, the voice of sanity at the other end of the line, a friend who is always willing to listen to a whine or celebrate a victory. Thanks, girl. I don't remember how I got by without you.

Thanks also go to Karen Harbaugh for details on Washington State. Any mistakes are, of course, my own.

Prologue

Forever after, he saw the explosion in slow motion.

First, the low evening sunlight, glowing on the pale ancient stone of the bridge and glittering over the water of the Seine. Next to him, the freshly lipsticked mouth of his lover, Marguerite, curled in a teasing smile as she reached for the crook of his arm. Ahead of them walked Julian "Jules" Moreau, dressed as always in a sleek Italian suit, his hair combed back into a ponytail to increase his resemblance to an American film star.

All three were operatives for the Organization, a private, top-secret peacekeeping agency, but this soft July evening they were free, their bellies satisfied with good wine and tender veal served by one of the finest chefs in Paris. For one small moment, Zane allowed himself to marvel over the fact that a mixed-blood Blackfoot man from a tiny Colorado town was walking in this famous, rose-gold light on a street a thousand years old. The wine they'd drunk at dinner had filled his veins with a lazy, rich sense of peace, and he glanced down at Marguerite and smiled a promise. She lifted an eyebrow wickedly and snuggled a little closer. They would go to Zane's flat, a second-floor walk-up with long windows that afforded views of the rooftops of the City of Light, as romantic a sight as any he'd seen.

From behind them came a shout, and Zane glanced over his shoulder to see the waiter, smiling and waving him back, holding up Zane's linen jacket. With a rueful laugh, he patted Marguerite's hand and returned back to fetch it.

One step, two. His heels clicked on the old pavement.

Then a ripple of warning ripped up the back of his neck, triggered by something caught from the corner of his eye. Urgently, Zane whirled to cry out a warning: ''Don't—''

Too late. Jules raised his head, but his hand was already lifting the door handle, and the car, expertly wired, exploded in a shattering, shrapnel-ridden blaze. Zane saw the flame, the noxious black cloud, an instant before he was slammed to the ground, feeling his leg give way under the weight of something he could not see. His breath whooshed from his lungs.

Seeping blackness bled into his vision, and he had only a moment to realize Marguerite and Julian had been destroyed by that inferno, before unconsciousness claimed him.

Chapter 1

Claire Franklin put her hands on her hips and narrowed her eyes at the load on top of her heavy-duty sports utility vehicle. The tree was seven feet of sweet-smelling fir, purchased from a local Christmas tree farmer who'd been happy to tie it to the roof for her at his lot. And on her roof it remained. She scowled at it, already feeling the tangle of panic crowding out the air in her chest. She hadn't considered the problem of getting it off the truck and into the house by herself.

Still, there was no one else. She made a stab at the task, first untangling the ropes laced through the branches, and discovered an unfortunate fact: the tree was very prickly. The bark was also sticky with sap, and when she pulled her hand away, reddish-brown flakes stuck to the golden resin on her palms.

"Yuck," she said aloud, and bent over to wipe her hand in the grass. Not that it did much good. The minute she put her hand amid those branches and started to tug the tree carefully off the top of the truck, the stuff was all over her hands again.

And there were—ugh—spiders living in its branches. One crawled right over her hand and nearly up her coat sleeve before she figured out that it wasn't just a branch tickling her. With a yelp, she yanked her hand away, shuddering, and the tree crashed to the ground, nearly squishing her dog, Coach, who skittered out of the way just in time.

The young shepherd gave her a wounded look. Claire, still shaking the spider creeps from her hands, said, "I didn't do it on purpose." She shuddered violently. "Gross. I hate spiders."

At least the mishap got the tree off the roof of the truck. Pulling her coat sleeves down over her hands to protect against any other lurking creatures, Claire gingerly stuck her arm down between the glossy needles and gripped the top of the trunk. She pulled. It didn't budge. She yanked hard, grunting with the weight, feeling the strain in her shoulders. But the tree moved—reluctantly—across the wet grass.

Naturally, the leaden skies chose just that moment to commence their weeping. It wasn't a heavy rain, at least not yet, but the drizzle added to her sense of martyred misery, soaking her hair and running beneath the collar of her coat.

Grimly, Claire kept at it and dragged the tree across the yard toward her pretty, freshly painted bed-and-breakfast, cursing under her breath. "I hate Christmas. I hate Christmas trees. I hate all this hassle for one stupid day of the year."

But that was not entirely true. She genuinely wanted to like the holiday. She loved Christmas carols and the smell of baking cookies. But nothing made her feel so much a fake as a holiday she'd never really celebrated as a child.

Puffing, she made it to the edge of the lawn and paused to give her lower back a rest. Drizzle washed her face, and she blotted it with the inner sleeve of her lined flannel jacket.

It would be different if she could claim exemption from the holiday on religious or cultural grounds. It wasn't, after all, as if everybody on the planet celebrated Christmas. For millions of Hindus and Buddhists and Muslims, it was a plain old ordinary day.

Coach sniffed the tree curiously. Claire rubbed his wheat-colored ears, taking the same pleasure she always did in the velvety softness. Dog ears were one of the great blessings of life. "I could convert," she said to him. "Then I'd never have to worry about it again." He looked up and wagged his tail, then went back to sniffing the branches. "You're right. Silly idea."

The rueful conversation with herself made her feel marginally better, and she told herself to be grateful for what she did have, instead of whining about what she didn't. A dog, for one thing. She'd not been able to have one in years, and aside from the sweetness of his ears, he was a good companion. People thought you were a lot less crazy if you talked to an animal instead of yourself, though she'd personally never seen much difference.

With a sigh, she bent down and grabbed the tree and started dragging it again. She told herself she could do this—not just get it inside, but make it beautiful. She had learned to create the illusion of home for her guests at the inn in every other way. Her simple, home-style food was a big lure, and she'd decorated the rooms with the kind of warmth and comfort she'd dreamed of as a child. How hard could decorating a Christmas tree be?

Except none of those other things disarmed her like Christmas did. She loved to cook and shop for the guest rooms, and decorating was one of her few serious talents. She had an eye for color and balance, and enough imagination to enjoy the challenge of reproducing expensive effects on a shoestring.

Only Christmas still had the power to unsettle her.

During her seven years at a large hotel chain, Christmas had always been a very businesslike affair, and someone else was always in charge of decorating.

Last year, her first at the inn, she had not had to cope with it at all, as the season had not brought guests to her new home. She'd thought, until two days ago, that she would slide by the same way this year. A large group of elderly German tourists had left yesterday, and starting in January, there were plenty of bookings, but the three weeks in between had been blissfully clear. Happily, she'd thought she would escape the need for a tree or decorations or anything else to do with the holiday. Instead, she'd planned to give the inn a good cleaning, and get her taxes done early.

Two days ago a reservation had come in, ruining that little scenario. One guest wouldn't change her holiday plans that much; she could still clean and do taxes. Except that she felt obligated to erect a Christmas tree now. What good innkeeper did not have a beautiful Christmas tree set up the week before Christmas?

Stopping to rest at the foot of the porch steps, she straightened and rubbed the small of her back. The tree, dark green and fragrant, stretched out behind her, the ultimate symbol of all Claire had missed, and no matter how much she gave herself pep talks, the sight of it gave her a strange, sad twist in her gut.

Coach suddenly gave a sharp, loud bark and took off into the forest that edged her property. "Coach!" she cried, annoyed. "You are never going to catch that squirrel! Get back here!"

He ignored her, as he always did, and she heard him racing around in the trees with exuberant excitement. He wouldn't go far, and the inn was isolated enough that he was in no danger. Once she got the tree inside, she could whistle him back home.

With a heavy sigh, she grasped the tree again and started the long process of hauling it up the stairs. It was a lot harder than she'd anticipated. The grass had been wet, so the tree had slid over it almost effortlessly. Now she had to haul its weight up the stairs. She groaned with effort, and at the top step paused again, breathing hard as she clung to the top of the tree with a shaky arm.

A voice shattered the still, rainy quiet. "Need help?"

Claire gave a startled cry and dropped the tree. It slid immediately down the stairs. Because her balance had been in tandem with the tree, she stumbled with it, landing with no small indignity on her rear in the wet grass. She swore, and not with ladylike mildness.

The man who'd spoken stepped close, and Claire's eyes went from feet to face in an instant, gathering details in an old, defensive habit, born in a childhood spent in neighborhoods where a child might encounter a drunk or a dangerous felon or any number of other frightening possibilities at any moment.

What she saw was not reassuring. He was tall and almost too lean, as if he'd had hard times recently, an impression reinforced by the jeans he wore. They were

worn to an ancient sky blue, and his left knee, brown
and smooth, showed through a tear. The other leg was
laced up the side with rawhide, to make room for a
cast that went from ankle to thigh. She raised her eyes.
Dark sunglasses and the brim of a Toronto Blue Jays
hat obscured most of his face, and his mouth was utterly without expression. Not mean, but not smiling.

Claire felt a sense of warning. He looked hard. And
dangerous, and not at all the kind of guest ordinarily
attracted to her cozy B and B.

Warily, Claire stood, lifting her chin. "May I help
you?"

"Looks like you're the one who needs help." The
voice was deep as a canyon.

"I'll be all right," she said briskly. "If you're looking for—"

"I made a reservation."

"Oh." Startled, she frowned and glanced at her
watch. "I didn't expect you for another three or four
hours."

"Things went more smoothly than I expected." His
accent was unusual, cultured, with a faint lilt that she
associated with western Native American tribes. "I assumed there would be no trouble."

"Oh, no. Not at all." Flustered by her own rudeness,
she stuck out her hand. "Claire Franklin."

He shifted his cane to his left hand and took hers in
his right. It was a strong hand, lean and dark and very
large. "Zane Hunter." He paused. "The reservation is
under Don Jones. My uncle reserved it for me."

His smooth delivery and manners could not entirely
cancel the impression of danger, and Claire found she
was bothered by his sunglasses. You could tell more
about a person if you could see his eyes. "Will you

please remove your sunglasses, Mr. Hunter? It's disconcerting to talk to myself in twin mirrors.''

"My apologies," he said, and raised one long-fingered hand to take off his glasses, then took off the hat, too. "Better?"

Lord have mercy. Claire heard the words in her mother's smoky drawl, for this was exactly the kind of man Larissa would have sidled up to. His eyes were as green as pine, his hair black and shiny as a seal's back. It spilled over his shoulders in an extravagant fall, the kind of hair only a Native American man could get away with past the age of twenty.

Claire's mother would have loved that hair. And his mouth. And his size. Most of all, she would have swooned over the look in his eyes—hooded but alluring, distant but inviting.

Oh, yeah. Larissa would have been all over this guy.

But Claire, thank heaven, was not her mother. "Much better," she replied, and evenly met his eyes. She gestured toward the ramp to one side. "Let me take your pack."

For a moment, he didn't reply, looking from the ramp to the tree. "Just a question—why did you try to haul the tree up the steps instead of going up the ramp?"

Claire blinked. *Because I'm an idiot and was having a panic attack,* she thought. Aloud, she said, "I have no idea. I wasn't thinking."

"I can't help you a hell of a lot with this cast on my leg, but we can probably get it inside between the two of us." Without waiting for a reply, he gracefully tossed his pack onto the relatively dry porch, then went to the top of the tree. "You take hold at the base. Better leverage that way."

"Oh." Of course. There wouldn't even be spiders at that end. She bent over and grabbed it with both hands, then started to pull. At the other end, the man stuck his hands between the branches and pushed. His posture was awkward, but he moved surprisingly easily in spite of it. Inside three minutes, they'd scooted the tree over the grass and up the ramp and into the wide foyer.

Sincerely, Claire said, "Thank you."

"Any time," he said, brushing his hands together, but Claire suddenly saw the white around his mouth, the lines of strain around the seductive eyes.

"Would you like something to eat, Mr. Hunter? I made soup for dinner, since I was not sure when you would arrive."

He leaned on his cane. "Please. I've come a very long way today."

"Oh?" she answered politely. "How far?"

"About five thousand miles, give or take a hundred."

She glanced at the T-shirt with its French slogan and made a guess. "Paris?"

He only nodded, his gaze sliding away. Hiding something.

Claire took the hint and didn't press any further. She led him into the dining room and got him settled in a wing chair that looked out over the back garden through a double set of French doors. In summer, the view was serene and colorful. At the moment, there were no flowers outside, but the trees in the forest were appealing, and she had giant pots of ferns and impatiens blooming inside. Some of her shattered confidence seeped back. "Make yourself comfortable," she said. "I'll be right back."

Humming under her breath, she ladled hearty vegetable beef soup into a thick ceramic bowl and arranged freshly baked slices of a nutty bread on a plate. She ducked her head into the fridge for a tiny bowl of butter shaped into a neat round. The phone rang. Carrying the butter to the tray, Claire picked it up. "Sea Breeze Bed and Breakfast, Claire Franklin speaking."

"Hallo!" The voice was light and feminine, unmistakably accented with French. "Have you any rooms available?"

Two last-minute reservations in a week—from France? Odd. "I can almost certainly accommodate you, ma'am. How many people and when?" She tucked the phone between her shoulder and ear and settled a heavy ceramic cup on the tray, wondering if her guest would prefer coffee or tea or something like an herb tea. She glanced at him through the doorway. Coffee. She'd lay money on it. Probably black coffee.

"Tomorrow?" The woman said. "A single room."

"That would be no problem at all." She quoted a price.

"Ah, so inexpensive! Very good. Let me check my last site and I will call you back."

"No problem." Claire hung up and carried the tray in to her guest. "I took a chance that you'd like coffee. If you prefer, I have teas of all sorts."

He roused himself. "Coffee is great. Thanks."

"Cream or sugar?"

"No," he said, "I take it black."

Claire smiled. She was very rarely wrong.

Although he tried to keep his shell firmly in place, Zane was so exhausted he could barely breathe. After six months of enforced recovery in the south of France, he'd pushed hard the past twenty-four hours, and his broken body screamed in protest. He hurt in places he ordinarily never thought about—in the repaired joint of his left elbow, in the healed cracks of his left ankle. About the only place that didn't hurt was his right leg, encased in its protective cast. That, naturally, itched. Two more weeks and the damned cast came off.

After he ate, the woman led him to a ground-floor room with the same view as the dining room. He followed her numbly down the hall, smelling something vaguely spicy, maybe potpourri, and the rich undernotes of pine on his hands.

The woman, like her inn, was an unexpected relief. She was small and ordinary, her presence as soothing as the hearty soup she'd served him. She hadn't chattered or fluttered, only seen to his comfort in sure, honest ways. No trouble.

She opened a door and stood back to let him pass. "Here you are."

He moved by her into the room. Like everything else about the place, it insisted upon relaxation, coaxed Zane's guard into pleased insensibility. A very dangerous state, considering his circumstances, but he was too exhausted to worry about it at the moment.

He nodded. "Perfect," he said, and looked back at her. Her gaze slid away guiltily, in a way that made him understand she'd been staring at him.

And for the first time, he noticed she was pretty. Not in the painted, polished way of the women who'd been in his life the past ten years. No, she wore little makeup on her clear, even features, and the long, honey-colored hair was tied back from her face in an artless ponytail. Jeans and a lightweight turtleneck showed small, pretty breasts and a tiny waist.

To his surprise, a faint thread of attraction wound through him. She gestured toward the attached bathroom and the neat stacks of towels, and he found himself remembering what female flesh felt like, that warmth and the scent, the round of a bottom in his palm.

"You should find everything you need, but please don't hesitate to ask for anything you require," she said. "Is there anything else I can get for you?"

"No, thanks."

She smiled. "Sweet dreams."

Standing alone in his room, Zane exhaled heavily and dropped his cane to the floor. Without even bothering to take off his shoes, he fell face first on the bed and closed his eyes. A curious sense of relief washed through him, relief as vast and irresistible as a mother's lullaby. He smelled rain and starch and the lingering scent of soup. His body relaxed.

There was a lot ahead of him still, but the first stage of his plan had been completed. Here, in this isolated inn, he could rebuild his strength. Hone his skills so he could, at last, have his revenge.

With the wisps of a woman's smile lingering against his eyelids, the soft sound of rain in his ears, he fell into a sleep as deep and sound as that of a boy.

Embarrassed by her clumsiness earlier, Claire was determined to have the tree up and decorated by the time her guest awakened the next morning. She didn't like the idea of appearing less than competent at something as simple as tree decorating.

But it took nearly an hour to figure out the tree stand and the logistics of getting the enormous tree upright—until the obvious trick of putting the stand on the prone

tree occurred to her. Pleased with her solution, she
tightened the little screws around the trunk, then had
to figure out how to stand the tree up by herself. It
wasn't, she realized, a one-person job.

Still, she managed to do it by rigging up a pulley
out of ropes and a plant hook. That accomplishment
pleased her so mightily that she decided to go whole
hog and create a Christmas world for herself. She put
a pot of apple-spice potpourri on the back of the stove
to simmer, and popped in a brand-new CD of Christmas music, keeping the volume low so as not to disturb
her guest. Outside, as if nature wanted to contribute to
her cause, the rain turned to thick, iridescent snow.
Admiring it through the windows, Claire chuckled to
herself.

"I can do this," she said to Coach, who obligingly
wagged his tail, then fell back into a deep sleep.

The brand-new boxes of ornaments, lights and various extraneous decorations were piled up against the
wall. Even Claire knew from decorating school Christmas trees in her youth that the lights had to go on first,
and she tackled that task with a ladder and the sound
of "God Rest Ye Merry Gentlemen" in her ears. The
carol made her feel happy and she sang along cheerfully, remembering concerts and performances at various shopping centers and nursing homes through high
school. Those trips had often been the highlight of her
season.

She got the lights on and felt a fluttery little joy when
she plugged in the cord and the tiny, multicolored bulbs
blinked on in perfect balance on the branches. "Ha!"
she said. "This isn't so hard."

Next step. She wrapped thick, sparkly garlands of
red and gold and purple over the branches. They were

her one extravagance, to please the child in her who had gazed longingly at them in magazines and store-fronts.

She'd chosen ornaments with a Victorian theme in mind—small wooden apples and decoupage balls and pretty little angels and a box of long glass tubes. As she was hanging the last of them, the phone rang again. Startled, Claire looked at the clock. Just past midnight. Who could be calling so late? With a sense of fore-boding, she rushed to the kitchen set, and answered, "Sea Breeze Bed and Breakfast."

A silence met her words, but it had the quality of connection, so Claire paused a moment before hanging up. A woman's voice, heavily accented, said, "Hallo? Is this the Sea Breeze inn?"

"Yes." Another French caller. "May I help you?"

"I hope so." A musical little laugh traveled over the wire, and Claire thought of the bubbles in champagne. "I have had so much trouble—how do you say it?—getting through!"

"I'm sorry. How may I help?"

"I'm looking for my cousin, who might be staying with you. Hunter?"

Three different people connected to France in one day? Little bit too much to lay at the feet of coinci-dence. For no reason she could name, a frisson of warning rippled down Claire's spine. "I'll be glad to take a message," she said evasively. Often her guests chose the inn for its privacy.

"Oh, has he not yet arrived?" There was a pout to the words. "I wanted to wish him a happy Christmas."

Claire frowned at the petulant sexiness in the voice. Some cousin. She remembered the French T-shirt Zane Hunter had worn and the five-thousand-mile journey he'd made. Maybe the woman was the reason for the long flight. A persistent and unwanted lover, perhaps. "As I said, ma'am, I'd be happy to take a message if you'd like to leave your name and number."

"No, no. I'll catch up later." The connection terminated.

Claire hung up, bothered. She made a mental note to mention the call casually and watch for his reaction. If there was going to be domestic trouble, Claire wanted to be prepared. In the meantime, she would not disturb the obviously exhausted man with a phone call.

Brushing it off, she headed back to the tree—and stopped in the doorway, her heart plummeting.

The tree looked ridiculous. She'd thought she'd done it so perfectly, but it didn't look at all like a picture in a magazine. Not even as good as the paper-snowflake-hung trees in her childhood classrooms.

It looked stupid. And for the life of her, Claire didn't know what to do to fix it. As she stared at it, a bleak sense of loss overwhelmed her, and she sank down in a chair and did something she never allowed: she put her head in her hands and began to weep.

Chapter 2

Zane surfaced in a dark room, his body stiff and cold. For a moment, he couldn't remember where he was or when it was, or what that smell in his nose might be. His training kept him motionless while he figured it out. Not the hospital. Not the hotel where he'd spent the night before. His clothes were still on, even his coat, and the bed smelled of starch. Distantly, a phone rang, and Zane heard the soft voice of a woman answer.

Details clicked in—the airport in Seattle, the ferry ride across Puget Sound to this small island and the quaint bed-and-breakfast. Blinking, he lifted his head. Darkness shrouded the room, and he could tell by the twist of his shirt that he'd been sleeping in his clothes for several hours.

Made awkward by the cast and stiff from so many hours in cramped airline seats, he got up and made his way to the bathroom. A cheery bright light over the vanity illuminated his face. "Damn, man," he said, stepping closer to assess the damage. The journey showed in ways it never would have ten years ago, putting lines of weariness around his mouth, drawing the flesh over his cheekbones taut. He rubbed his lightly stubbled jaw. Getting old, he thought with a shake of his head. The kind of life he'd been living made a man old long before his time, and Zane had a feeling his clock had started ticking triple time.

A shower would help. He stripped off his clothes and left them in a pile on the floor. With careful maneuvering to keep the cast dry, he managed to get a decent shower. It helped. The soap smelled like a forest and the shampoo like a sea, and the towels were thick and expensive.

Whistling, he shaved and dressed—not a lot of choices but jeans and T-shirts, since he'd had to pack light—then went in search of his hostess, hoping to get a cup of the coffee he could smell.

Only when he was in the hall did he stop to wonder what time it might be. His body was still on Paris time. It might be really late. But the house didn't feel like it was sleeping. He could hear music coming from somewhere, and the lights were still on. He felt good for the first time in three days, and the coffee smelled like ambrosia. He'd just ask about the coffee, and see if there was someplace to watch a little American television for a while—try a taste of the ordinary for a change.

He passed a spacious room, where a fire burned cheerfully in the grate. Through wide arched windows, Zane saw snow falling in thick starry flakes, and Christmas carols played softly in the background. He smiled. The place was like a movie set. Any minute now, the dogs and kids would come rushing into the room, along with Hilda Housewife in her holiday dress and stockings, and Joe Dad with his pipe and slippers. Who knew such places still existed?

In spite of the cynical thought, he was reminded, ever so faintly, of a kind of Christmas feeling he'd not experienced in years. A sensory memory of the taste of frosted butter cookies and the smell of his mother's talcum powder and the sound of church suppers sailed through him, bringing with it a powerful wave of emotion. For one split second, he wondered why he hadn't just gone home for Christmas this year. Or the years before, for that matter.

Then, with a shake of his head, he dismissed the idea as foolish nostalgia. If he had gone home, his mother would have fussed and worried over him, clicking her tongue over the weight he'd lost, asking a million questions about his injuries—questions he simply could not answer. Instead, he'd sent silk scarves and Swiss chocolate and the English tea his mother loved so much. She would share the booty with her church ladies, and brag about his glamorous job that took him to faraway places. Much better for her if he stayed away.

His stomach growled, and shaken from his reverie, he moved toward the kitchen. Halfway there, he paused, hearing a faint sound. Crying?

With a frown, he edged quietly toward the dining room, where he'd eaten his soup, and carefully, so as not to intrude on her privacy, peeked around the corner.

The woman who had made him so comfortable sat in an overstuffed chair, her knees drawn up in front of her, her head in her arms. Zane found his attention snared by a single loose tendril of hair that fell over her elbow, a glossy honey color, soft as a child's.

And she wept like a child, not a child who was petulant or tired, but one who had been deserted by everyone. There was a heartbroken, despairing sound to it that pierced him. It was lonely. So sad.

He remembered that the phone had awakened him and wondered if she'd had bad news. Before he knew he would do it, he entered the room and said to her, "Hey, are you all right?"

She made a soft, choked sound and looked up. "Oh! Uh...I, uh, I'm sorry." She covered her face with one hand, shielding herself from his gaze. Her cheeks shone with her tears, and her eyelashes were spiked to long, triangular points. She wiped ineffectively with her hand before she rubbed a sleeve beneath one eye, then the other. Like a little girl. "Sorry," she said again.

"You didn't wake me."

"Good." She started to duck away. "Can I get you—"

Zane put a hand on her arm. "Is there something I can do?"

She raised her eyes. He had been too zonked to notice before, or maybe the tears had lent the color intensity, but they were eyes of a wildly beautiful turquoise, and in their depths he saw a flickering of emotions—embarrassment, maybe, and helplessness, and resolve, and oddly, despair.

"It's nothing. It's stupid."

"What is?"

With a hand inside her sleeve, she gestured toward the corner. "The tree."

Zane looked. "Oh."

She'd managed to get it straight, but that was about the only good thing Zane could see. The beautiful seven-foot fir was as gaudily dressed as a ten-cent whore.

"You see? I don't know what I did wrong." Her expression was far bleaker than the situation warranted.

"Yeah." He hesitated, his instincts warring with logic. He ought to just shrug it off, get some of that coffee and something to eat, and return to his room, where he could start plotting the next step in his plan for revenge.

Maybe it was the tug of the emotions he'd glimpsed in her tearful gaze. Or maybe he was softened by the season and the fleeting thought of his mother. Whatever it was, Zane surprised himself by saying, "Tell you what, if you'll get me some of that coffee I smell, I think I can help."

"No, that's okay. I didn't...I don't...you shouldn't—"

He cocked his head toward the kitchen. "Go on. Trust me."

Still subdued, she headed for the kitchen. Zane watched her for a moment, the small, straight shoulders, that tiny waist, and something he'd missed before: an absolutely gorgeous, heart-shaped rear end. Some might have said it was disproportionate, but he had a weakness for a generous derriere.

And it had been a very long time since he'd been with a woman. As if in approval, he felt a stirring in his nether regions, that leap of interest a man could never quite quell.

Don't even think about it, man. While it was good to see that his libido was returning, it would be a very bad idea to sleep with a sweet little innkeeper who cried over poorly decorated Christmas trees. A bit too vulnerable for his tastes.

A dog, a young shepherd mix by the look of him, stretched with a lazy groan on the floor by the tree. Zane squatted, the cast thrust out to one side, and scrubbed his belly for him. The dog roused slightly, opening one brown eye halfway and giving Zane a lick on the wrist before falling back into a deep sleep.

"He was chasing squirrels this afternoon," the woman said as she returned. She carried two heavy ceramic mugs, and gave him one.

"You know," Zane said, "I've been hoping it would come back to me, but it hasn't. I can't remember your name."

She smiled. "Claire."

Even a sweet name. "Got it. Sorry about that."

"You were pretty tired when you got here." She took a breath. "So, tell me, what did I do wrong with this thing?"

"Too much stuff." Carefully, he removed some long glass ornaments. "These are pretty, and I like the apples, but a lot of the rest can probably just come off." He plucked at the mufflers of red and gold. "Probably only need one or two of these."

"Oh." She crossed her arms.

He continued to remove items as he talked. Five tinsel ropes, leaving two. Seven garish plastic red ornaments. The apples, which he put in a box to put back on in a little while. The elegant glass tubes he nestled carefully in their own container. "My grandmother had some like this," he said, holding up a hand-painted, old-fashioned-style glass bulb. "Are they antiques?"

"No. It's all brand-new."

And she didn't know how to make it look right. He gave a nod, resisting the impulse to find out more. The less he found to interest him, the better. It wouldn't kill him to help a lady in distress for ten minutes, but going any further was off-limits.

"The trick," he said, "is to balance everything. Not too much of any one thing or one color." He hung a blue glass globe on one side, then hung another high up. "Like that." He stepped back, plucked a long tube from the box and gave it to her. "You try."

The night was dark and cold. The woman, dressed in black insulated ski pants and a fur-lined coat, did not feel it particularly. The snow annoyed her for practical reasons. It obscured the view, requiring her to leave the cover of the forest and break across virgin snow, leaving tracks. Since there was little chance anyone would see her, she shrugged the detail away.

In the deep shadows cast by an ancient monkey tree, she crouched, taking measure of the inn. A bank of mullioned windows fronted the central room, lit from within, and she saw figures moving—only blurs of color at this distance.

It was a rambling, old-fashioned place. On one side of the central room was another room, which she surmised would be the kitchen, lit with an overhead fluorescent. On the other side were double-hung windows, all dark. Probably guest rooms. Upstairs, one room was lit. She scowled. It would be more difficult if her quarry was nestled away on the second floor.

Soundless and wraithlike, she moved closer, no more substantial than the shadows of wind-tossed trees. The multipaned glass of the central room would make aim difficult, and she eyed the surrounding grounds for a better position. Light as the wind, she circled the house. Then she settled, patient as a tiger, to wait for her chance. Tonight, luck was with her. Tonight, Zane Hunter would die.

Standing in front of the Christmas tree, Claire hesitated, torn between wanting to please the man holding out an ornament like an offering to her and the fear that she'd still get it wrong. Abruptly, she took it from him and put it carefully on a branch. She was pleased beyond all reality when he said "Good," in that husky, somehow musical voice.

She glanced up, feeling a surge of gratitude. He was standing close, and Claire had to look a long way up, up and up, until she was snagged—hard—by the pine green eyes.

And for the space of a held breath, she forgot everything. Forgot the tree and the new ornament in her hand and the snow beyond the window; forgot she had a taste for stable, ordinary men who would enjoy puttering in the yard; forgot that she had a lick of sense.

She forgot it all in the discovery that she had never, in all her born days, seen a face so beautiful. It was almost unreal, like a photograph or sculpture. His features were cleanly, artfully carved. His mouth was cut almost unbearably right for the shape of kisses. His brows formed a winged arch across a broad, intelligent brow. And falling with a heaviness that moved like water, his thick black hair framed the angles and curves. It was hair few women would be able to resist twining around their fingers.

Stung, Claire felt something rip free in her chest, as if her heart had suddenly taken the shape of a bird and begun to beat its wings against the cage of her ribs, as if it had been sleeping there until now, waiting for this moment, for those eyes.

A smile edged onto his mouth. A very seductive smile. Knowing.

And more than that. She saw with surprise that the seductiveness was softened with gentleness. It didn't nullify the secrets she had sensed in him earlier, or the wariness, but whatever life had made him, some woman had taught him to be gentle.

"Are you going to help?" he asked.

With a start, Claire realized that she was mooning at him like a teenager. Or her mother.

And like her mother, she was making him into a passion poem of heroic nobility. Flushing, she looked away. Though the world never seemed to get it, Claire understood quite clearly that handsome did not necessarily equal good. In fact, quite the opposite was generally true. The prettier the face, the blacker the heart.

By that measure, he probably cannibalized children. "I'm helping," she said, realizing she was still holding an ornament.

"Not so tough, once you get the knack of it." He turned from her to hang an angel from a high branch.

"Not at all," she said, and was pleased at the even, dignified sound of her voice. After a long, quiet space, filled with threads of a Christmas carol, she asked politely, "Are you from around here, Mr. Hunter?"

"Colorado, originally. A little town outside Denver."

"You didn't want to go home for Christmas?"

With one long-fingered brown hand, he pushed a lock of blackest hair from his face and stepped back to narrow his eyes as he looked at the tree. "No. I've been away a long time."

"All the more reason."

He lifted a shoulder. "I have some things to do before I can go home." His mouth looked a little grim.

"Ah." Respecting his privacy, Claire picked up a box of icicles. "Is there a trick to these, too?"

He turned, and with a very slow smile, said, "They go on one at a time."

The smile tilted his eyes slightly, and made the high slope of cheekbones more prominent and showed straight white teeth. Even more, it brought an impish, sexy light to his eyes, a look that promised he understood the concept of enjoyment very well. "Oh," Claire said, feeling that bird move and flutter inside of her, moving into her breasts, under her flesh.

He tore the plastic from the package and gathered a hank of tinsel. "Like this," he said, and illustrated.

There was something elegant about the airy silver tinsel cascading over the graceful elegance of his dark hand. Claire admired it for a long moment before she realized what she was doing—again!—then shook her head in bemusement.

Taking a handful of icicles from the box, she moved to the other side of the tree where she couldn't see him, and carefully draped them one at a time. "Oh," she said. "Like spiderwebs!"

"Right."

Through the branches, she could see the edge of his clean, carved jaw and part of his mouth. He was just short of perfect. What woman *wouldn't* notice? She used her head when it came to acting on her attractions, but that didn't mean she didn't feel them. Being careful didn't mean she was dead.

It had been a long day. She'd been emotionally upset in a way she hadn't experienced for many years, and he'd been kind to her. It was natural to be attracted to kindness.

It made her feel better, and she hummed along tunelessly to "Deck the Halls" on the CD player. "By the way," she said. "You had a phone call a little while ago."

Was the sudden stillness her imagination? "A caller for me?"

"Yes. Not more than an hour ago."

"That's impossible," he said flatly.

"Well, obviously not as impossible as you think." No, she was not imagining the stillness. It lay along his shoulders and in the careful tilt of his head, in the sudden looseness of his hands at his sides—like a man getting ready to draw a gun.

Her guard went up. "She wouldn't leave her name, but she asked for you."

"She?"

"Yes. French, I think. She said she was your cousin and she just wanted to tell you 'happy Christmas.'"

"I don't have any French cousins. Not even French-Canadian."

Claire hadn't considered that possibility, but she nodded. "I guessed it might be someone other than a cousin," she said dryly.

His mouth was hard. "Did you tell her I was here?"

"No. She wanted to know if you'd arrived yet. I ducked the question and told her I'd take a message."

"Good. For future reference, I'm not here, okay?"

"No problem." It wasn't an unusual request. Often people came to an island as isolated as this to get away from problematical relatives—or, as she suspected was the case here—a persistent lover. "As long as it isn't the police who call me."

"It's not like that."

"Good." She wondered, briefly, what he was hiding, but she said only, "Then your privacy is safe with me, Mr. Hunter."

"Call me Zane."

"Zane." Naturally he had a wild and unusual and romantic name. No man who looked like this was ever named Harry. "Is that your real name?" she asked impulsively.

"Believe it or not, it is. My mother had a thing for the writer Zane Grey." He glanced at her. "Uh, you have an icicle stuck to you." He gestured across his chest.

Claire looked down and saw the silvery strand crossing her breasts, almost exactly nipple to nipple. For some reason she didn't articulate even in her own mind, it embarrassed her to reach up and take it away. "Thanks," she said.

"No problem." The words were low and rich, redolent with a purely male note of appreciation.

She raised her chin and met the direct, deliberately seductive smile he gave her. It was a smile she'd seen a thousand times, as deceptive as the flash of a gambler's diamonds, meant to divert the unwary from the cards he was pulling from his sleeves. Behind it, she glimpsed the danger she had sensed when he first arrived, and she knew that her initial impression had been correct.

Zane Hunter was dangerous. Predator or prey?

She didn't know, and didn't care. She'd stay alert for the next day or two, and get rid of him on some pretext if necessary.

But she'd learned to hide her own thoughts, and gave him her best smile.

He quirked a brow quickly, then glanced back at the tree. "I think we're finished. How do you like it?"

"Looks good," Claire said.

He inclined his head in acceptance and smiled once more. "So, how about some more of that soup for my troubles?"

"Of course." She gestured to the kitchen. "I'll be right back."

As soon as she left the room, Zane swore under his breath and let the bleakness invade. Damn. He'd been so careful. How was it possible someone had tracked him down so quickly?

And more important, who?

He forced himself not to pace, to keep his face free of anything but the blandest of expressions, but he couldn't stand completely still. Restlessly, he moved toward the wide French doors and crossed his arms, looking out to the snowy, serene landscape.

The Organization did not know where he was. They would try to find him, he was sure, since the minute he went missing, his superiors would know he'd ignored the order that took the case out of his hands. Zane had protested furiously, but they'd been immovable, insisting the case had become too personal.

But they hadn't yet found him. A phone call made from an Ohio airport in the middle of the night had assured him of that.

The only other possibility was the Ghost himself. Damn.

The Ghost was an assassin, one of the most elusive and dangerous to operate since the Cold War. Invariably deadly and extremely well paid, he worked entirely alone, and was so mysterious it had taken years for various world intelligence agencies to realize there was a pattern. He preferred bombs, particularly the signature bomb that had killed Zane's associates, but he'd used nearly every method of murder known.

Zane had been assigned to the case eighteen months before the Paris car bomb, and he'd focused exclusively on tracking the assassin, going over every assassination attributed to him, reviewing police reports for missed details, inspecting the sites.

And by Christmas last year, Zane had been closing in. He'd begun to think like the Ghost, as he'd once been able to think like a deer in the woods, or the small lost boy whose successful rescue had led to Zane's current position. As he tracked the Ghost, he began to get a strong feeling for targets, too, the kind of cases the Ghost liked to take, and by luck, instinct and intelligence, Zane had managed to prevent the assassination of an African dignitary in Cairo last year. And then, two months later, a controversial Brazilian politician had missed being maimed because Zane had tracked the Ghost to Rio and defused an incendiary device in the man's hotel phone.

The Ghost had had his revenge on Zane in Paris six months ago. By now, he would know the main target had survived. By leaving the hospital, Zane hoped to draw him out, make himself a target and get his revenge for the death of his lover and his friend.

But he had not expected to be found so soon.

You had a phone call a little while ago…she asked for you.

She?

Yes. French, I think. She said she was your cousin and she just wanted to tell you happy Christmas.

Claire came into the room, humming off-key.

"Here's your soup," she said, putting the heavy, beautifully made ceramic bowl on the table.

"Do you have caller ID?" Zane asked.

"Yes." Wariness crept into her eyes. Suspicion.

Zane was glad. She might look like Mrs. Homemaker of America, but there was real grit in her manner. "Do you mind if I look at it?"

"Go ahead." She led him to the small box attached to a phone on the entry desk. "Since we're on the Sound, all but the island will be marked 'unavailable,' but sometimes there's a number, anyway."

"How many calls have you had this evening?" He took the box, but didn't yet press the button that would show him where the calls had originated.

"I don't know." She lifted a shoulder. Her arms were crossed over her chest. She didn't like this much at all. "Maybe four or five. Three for business, one inquiry about a room and the call from your—uh—cousin." She frowned. "What are you looking for, exactly?"

"I'm not sure." He punched the button and found a string of six "unavailables" in a row. When he pressed the button again, two of the six matched—the last one and one that had come in late this afternoon. A cold sense of warning chilled his spine. "What time did the call from my cousin come in?"

"About midnight, maybe?"

He found the log time. "Did she call more than once?"

"I don't think so." Then she looked puzzled. "Unless the French woman who called this afternoon was her, too."

"Look at the number," he said. "Do you know this area code?"

She leaned close. "It's local."

"And the prefix?"

Her voice was hushed. "On the island."

Worse than he had anticipated. Zane swore, and it wasn't a gentleman's word. The Ghost was not a very small man, as they had all believed.

He was a *she*.

Chapter 3

Claire looked up at him, turquoise eyes sober. "Is she dangerous?"

In the space of a breath, he decided not to lie if he could avoid it. "Maybe," he said evasively. She could assume it was an old lover, bent on revenge. "I have to get out of here. Now, or you'll be in danger, too."

She gave him a measured look, narrowing her eyes, but otherwise revealing nothing of her thoughts. "There isn't anywhere to go. There's no ferry till morning."

Zane looked around the room—the open drapes showing the gently falling snow, allowing anyone outside a clear view of those within. He thought of them decorating the Christmas tree in full view of those dark woods and felt faintly sick. "I'm going to close the drapes."

"I'll help."

"No." He bit out the word and saw the flare of

genuine fear in her eyes. He struggled with a way to soften it, and decided it wasn't possible. "Stay right where you are for a minute."

He limped to the back windows first and yanked the cords—first the filmy undercurtains, then a heavier, light-blocking set of drapes. When they were closed, he moved around the table methodically, watching where his shadow fell on the closed curtains. Only one light was problematic and he turned it off.

In the living room, he repeated the process, then nodded to Claire. "You can move now. I'm going to take care of the kitchen."

"No, wait!" Her voice was urgent. "There are no curtains. No blinds. Windows all the way around—and it faces the forest."

His estimation of her increased. She didn't know what was going on, but had guessed some of it. Good instincts. "Where's the switch for the light?"

"To the left of the door."

With a single nod, he moved toward the threshold. The house was perhaps eighty years old, and a pair of broad sliding doors were nested in the walls on either side of the kitchen. Hairs prickled on the back of his neck as he approached, seeing now the double-hung windows along the entire west wall. From outside, a sniper could—

The dog, sleeping until that moment, jumped up and barked loudly. Fiercely. Zane turned and made one long-armed swing as he dived for the floor, sweeping Claire beneath him. A volley of tiny pops echoed into the room over their heads, and Zane heard the dull ping of bullets hitting plaster.

Below him, Claire made a soft cry. He tightened his

grip on her shoulders, and growled, "Don't move, and don't scream."

She nodded rigidly.

The dog went into a frenzy, barking with a savage intensity, running toward the kitchen, then toward the back wall of windows, the French doors and the back-yard.

For the first time in years, Zane felt compelled to offer a prayer—not for his own safety, but for the innocent woman with him. He offered it silently, fervently, his hand protectively covering the silky crown of her head, his body as much a shield over her as he could manage.

"My dog!" she whispered urgently, shoving against him.

He held steady, but turned his head and whistled softly. The dog whined, cocking his head toward the door in a way that made Zane's hackles rise, as if there were someone just beyond.

But he didn't start barking again. For long, long moments, Zane held the woman beneath him, unmoving, his ears tuned to the smallest sounds, the slightest hint that the Ghost had not moved on, was only waiting to ambush them once they started moving.

Finally, he shifted his attention to the woman beneath him. He gripped her jaw and looked hard in her eyes. "Do exactly as I say and we might get out of this alive. Understand?"

She nodded, once, jerkily. There was not fear in her eyes but anger—no, a lot more than anger—pure, undiluted fury. Very good.

"You need your coat, your purse and your keys. Where are they?"

"In the closet." She yanked her chin out of his hands and nodded toward a door in the foyer.

"Stay close to the floor and get them as quietly as you can. Stay away from the windows and the kitchen doors. I have to get my pack from my room."

"The windows in there—"

"I know." He started to move, and she urgently pushed against him, suddenly making him worry that she would bolt the minute he let her go. He grasped her hard. "I swear you're in no danger from me, but if you tear out that door, you will be dead in three seconds. Get it?"

Mutiny flared and died. Her jaw went hard. "I get it."

He let her go and paused to make sure she was following instructions. In a crab walk, she edged toward the closet, raised a hand to gently open it and pulled a coat off a hanger. With a bitter little smile, she reached in the pocket for her keys and held them up. He gave her a nod, touched a single finger to his lips and made his way down the hall.

Claire held her coat against her and leaned her head back on the wall, expecting delayed reaction to set in. But, although her heart raced with adrenaline and she felt a rush of something hot in her belly, no wild sense of terror pushed through her. In the darkness of the foyer, she looked with dull eyes at the bullet holes in her living room wall and wondered how much it would cost to repair them.

While she waited, she put on the coat, a heavy down parka with a hood, and checked the pockets to make sure she had tissues. Cold weather made her nose run. When Zane had still not returned, she retied her shoes and reached into the closet for her purse. Too much trouble to carry the whole thing. Coldly, calmly, she unloaded its contents into her pockets—a brush, Chap Stick, half a pack of gum. The wallet was too bulky to fit, so she removed the driver's license, the single credit card and a handful of bills, and tucked them into the breast pocket of her coat, leaving the wallet on the floor.

Seeing her retie her shoes, Coach whined happily and trotted over, ready to go anywhere, any time. She rubbed his back. "Hang on, baby."

It reminded her of his leash, but if she reached up to get it off the closet hook, he'd go nuts, barking and whining and jumping all over. Instead, she rubbed his chest and stared at the wall gashes bleeding plaster dust to the floor.

Zane came back. Hobbled by the cast, he couldn't move quickly, and he came down the hall in a crouching limp, dragging his straight leg behind him. He'd put his hat on, pulled back his hair and donned a heavy coat he'd produced from only heaven knew where. The sturdy, expensive backpack was on his shoulder. He looked dangerously lean, as feral and beautiful as a wolf.

When he got to Claire, he knelt as well as he could in front of her. There was respect in his eyes, which moved her not at all. "Cool as a cucumber, aren't you?"

She met his gaze flatly. "We need extra blankets."

"All right. Where will I find them?"

"They're upstairs. I'll get them. You can't even walk properly."

He hesitated. "Go."

The stairs were in the protected center of the house.

Claire made her way to them, then stood up and dashed the rest of the way, feeling a monster prickle down her spine. Without turning on a light, she opened the linen closet, got out a pile of her warmest blankets, and paused.

Stealthily, she crept into her dark bedroom. The heavy cloud cover made it lighter outside, and she took advantage of that to peer carefully through the windows at the backyard.

No one was there, but the evidence that someone had been edged the garden, in a line of footprints. Going or coming? It was impossible to tell. With a bitter smile, she decided it didn't matter. The bullets proved there had been someone lurking outside.

Suddenly, she was not twenty-eight years old, looking out toward the serene landscape she'd chosen for herself, but thirteen, alone in the trailer she shared with her mother. The lights were off, and music played loudly from several trailers around her—'twas the season to be jolly, after all. In her lap, Claire cradled the telephone, her ears trained to the scrabbling sound of the drunk just beyond the thin, particleboard front door. Her throat was dry and her hands shook, but she wouldn't call 911 again unless he actually tried to get in.

A dog whined, and with an almost audible pop, Claire returned to the present. For one moment, she felt an unholy rage toward the man downstairs, for invading the safe world she'd made for herself, for sullying her sanctuary with bullets and the danger she'd scrambled so hard to escape.

But right now, anger was a luxury she couldn't afford. Right now, her best chance of staying safe was with the very man who'd put her in danger. Impul-

sively, she grabbed the pillows from her bed and
tucked a paperback book from the nightstand into another of her voluminous pockets. At the doorway, she
paused and looked over her shoulder, imprinting the
peace of the room in her mind. Then, with bitterness
in her mouth, she went back downstairs.

She didn't see Zane at first. With a little flutter of
hope, she wondered if he might have lit out into the
night without her. Then she saw him, the edge of his
shoulder and one arm and one long leg bordered with
light from the kitchen. He gestured, his long, graceful
hand fluttering into the light, and Claire carried her
burden of blankets over, kneeling beside him.

"Is your truck still parked in the same place it was
this afternoon?" he asked.

"No. I pulled it into the garage while you were
asleep."

"Excellent." His eyes glittered in the shadows. "As
you may have gathered, we're going to have to outrun
a sniper. I'd like it a hell of a lot better if I could drive,
but it isn't possible. Do you think you can do it?"

She nodded.

"We just need to get somewhere for the night, someplace isolated and dark, where our friend won't find us.
Then we'll get the ferry off the island first thing."

"We? You aren't going to let me go then?"

He looked away. "We'll see." From inside his
jacket, he withdrew an enormous gun, heavy and black
and dangerous. "Let's go."

For one small moment, Claire felt a wave of nau-
seous terror rush through her. "I hate guns," she said
quietly.

"Yeah," he said, "me, too." With a tilt of his head,
he nudged her along.

And there was really nothing else to do. Claire led the way to the door into the garage, which opened off the foyer. In the dark, she quietly opened the driver's side door, whistled softly and pulled back the seat for Coach, then unlocked the passenger door for Zane.

He got in, laboriously, and pushed back the seat to give room for the cast. "The only danger point will be the stretch between the garage and the road. You start the truck and I'll hit the garage door opener. Back out as fast as you can, all the way to the road."

Claire said, "I can't do that."

"What?"

"Back up fast. I can't see well enough."

"All right. Back out, then do whatever you have to do to get us down that driveway as fast as you can." He lifted his hand to the garage door opener on the visor. "Ready?"

"Yes."

"Keep your head down."

Again, a wave of nausea hit her. A dozen scenes from movies passed in front of her imagination, squealing tires, spidery breaks in windshields radiating from a tiny hole, the driver slumped and bleeding over the steering wheel while the car careened out of control. With a sense of panic, she wondered what would happen to Coach if she had an accident, and the thought made her grit her teeth and force the images away. She started the engine.

Zane hit the garage door opener, and when it was halfway up, he shouted, "Go!"

Claire gunned it, backward. The tires hit the slippery snow and spun a little. Blood rushed through her ears, roaring with the punch of adrenaline, and she braked jerkily, threw the vehicle into Drive and flicked on the lights, racing for the end of the driveway.

It looked like they'd escape unnoticed, but suddenly a ping hit the back of the sports utility vehicle, and Coach went into a barking frenzy. Terrified her dog had been shot, Claire slowed down, peering into the rearview mirror.

"Go!" Zane cried. *"Go!"*

Another shot pinged into the side of the car, and Claire realized the sniper was aiming for her tires. She stomped on the accelerator, barely slowing down for the turn to the main road. The truck lurched sickeningly as they hit a pothole and nearly overbalanced, but she gained control in a few seconds.

It wasn't much of a road. A slim dirt track, rutted and bumpy at the best of times, cut through the forest. The wet weather made it muddy and slippery. Claire hit the brights and slowed down to a manageable rate of speed to handle the twists and curves and sudden lurches, thankful for her four-wheel drive.

After a few minutes, they came to the paved road that led two miles into town and the dock. Claire halted at the stop sign. "Now what?"

"You know the island. Where can we hide for a few hours?"

Claire considered and discarded several possibilities, then turned decisively to the left. "I know a good place."

It wasn't far. Claire had discovered it over the summer, an overlooked track that led to a placid, protected spot on the beach. In the daytime in good weather, the Cascades rose in blue splendor and the Sound glittered with sunlight, but in spite of the view, Claire had never encountered another person there. Pilings from some old timber operation made it inaccessible for boats, even small ones, and the ghostly remainder of the mill was a haunting sight. She had always assumed people simply avoided it for that reason. Tonight, she didn't care. She pulled under the shelter of two towering firs and shut off the engine. "This is the best I can do."

"Excellent."

In the sudden silence, they sat side by side, staring at the water that undulated beneath the relentlessly falling snow. Claire let the view work its soothing effects on her nerves, feeling the jerky edge of adrenaline drain from her.

When she trusted herself to be calm, she said, "So, I'm guessing this isn't just your run-of-the-mill bad love affair."

"No."

When he added nothing, she narrowed her eyes. "I think you owe me some kind of explanation."

A pause. "I can't."

"You can't?" she repeated. "Or won't?"

"I'm not, as they say, at liberty to reveal that information."

Now she had the luxury of anger, and she let it go. "What are you, the FBI? CIA? A drug smuggler? If you tell me who you are and who the hell was shooting up my hotel, will someone come and remove my fingers one knuckle at a time?"

"No." The word was husky. Maybe a little ashamed. "The less you know, the better off you are."

"That's bull…crap," she retorted. "You sound like a bad movie."

"Sorry." He lifted his hat, then replaced it. "I know it sounds melodramatic. It also happens to be true." He finally looked at her. "What I can tell you is that

I'm on the right side of the law, and the sniper is on the wrong side. I came here to get my strength back so I could take on—'' He scowled. ''Take revenge. Somehow, I was followed.''

''How lucky for me,'' she said bitterly.

''I'm sorry.''

Suddenly winded, Claire shook her head. ''Whatever. No use crying over spilt milk.'' With an abrupt gesture, she opened her door and climbed into the back seat. ''I'm going to try to get some sleep.'' She handed him a blanket and a pillow. ''There's a lever on the side that will make that seat go back.''

''I'll keep watch,'' he said.

''You do that.'' She plumped up the pillow, shoved Coach out of her way and lay down, covering herself with the blanket. ''The ferry leaves the dock at five-fifteen, so we need to get out of here about quarter to.''

''Got it.''

She closed her eyes. It was utterly silent here, which seemed strange after the roaring in her ears the past hour. Coach put his head on the seat next to her and made a tiny begging noise. Needing the warmth of a living body to hold on to, she lifted the blanket and moved over to give him room to lie down beside her. It was a tight fit, but Claire didn't mind. She draped her arm around him. His furry body pressed against her chest and stomach, and his head rested on her arm. The seat cradled her back. Between them, she felt snug and secure. He sighed happily.

Claire rested her head against his neck. It was a familiar and comforting pattern, born in childhood. Her mother sometimes made it home at night and sometimes didn't, but Claire always had her dog—a midsize mongrel who slept with her every night. Holding on to

Jake, she'd never felt afraid. She could fall asleep without worry, knowing he'd never allow anyone inside without barking wildly, and he'd never let anyone hurt her. He'd also been warm, and he kept the loneliness at bay.

The same sense of safety seeped through her now. Comforted and warm, she fell into an exhausted slumber.

Zane kept watch, less out of a sense of danger than habit. He suspected the protected spot would be difficult to find unless someone knew where to look.

Time crawled in the dark silence. He watched water break on shore beneath the curtain of snow and felt something in him ease a little. It was a beautiful night. Faintly, he could see the Christmas lights at homes on another island not far away, and their cheery brightness eased the tense despair Zane felt creeping in.

The waves lapped at the shore with hypnotic regularity. It was cold, so he was in no danger of falling asleep, and the regular motion of nature eased him, cleared away extraneous details, and focused his thoughts. He particularly liked water for that purpose; something about the slap and rush of it, the sound. As a child and young man, his favorite thinking place had been on the banks of a sleepy river that ran nearly dry in the summer, and rushed with noise and fury through the spring.

He definitely needed to think now.

Keeping the Glock in hand, cold and heavy and reassuring, he reviewed every step he'd taken since his release from the hospital four days ago, trying to figure out how the Ghost had caught up to him so quickly. Zane had planned his disappearance very carefully, knowing those who would track him had the most sophisticated tools imaginable at their disposal. To cross international borders, he'd needed papers in assumed names, which he'd acquired through an elaborate network of mercenaries. He'd trusted them only as far as he could keep his eyes on them, and to be absolutely certain he'd not be betrayed, he'd had the papers made in three names by three different operators. At each stop on his journey to the States, he had changed airlines and identities, leaving a false paper trail designed to throw followers off his scent.

Even the method by which he'd chosen the inn itself had been utterly random. Days before he left the hospital, he'd made a trip to town, taken out an atlas and stabbed a finger down to find a geographical location. Then he'd used a terminal connection at the library to access the Internet and get a list of hotels in the area. The Sea Breeze name caught his imagination, and he memorized the phone number.

The low rumble of a plane disturbed the quiet, and Zane looked for lights he could not see through the clouds. Meditatively, he rubbed his thumb along the barrel of the Glock and pursed his lips in concentration.

Obviously, he'd slipped up somewhere. He'd made the reservation at the inn from an airport in New Jersey with a phone card in a name he'd used to get from Paris to New York.

The only other call he'd made had been to a trusted friend, and not even Max had known Zane's target destination or anything else that would have led the Ghost to him. Even if Max's phone was tapped—a distinct possibility, since they were known to be friends—Zane had revealed nothing about his plans. He wouldn't even have made that call, but in his weakened condition,

Zane might need backup, and the only man he could trust was Max Azul.

It had to be the IDs. Somehow, the Ghost had obtained the names and managed to track him here. She no doubt had a prodigious fortune at her fingertips; Zane supposed she could have discreetly advertised her wish to know if Hunter purchased false papers.

Except, he'd been very careful. He'd been in the business a long time. He didn't make foolish errors; he'd gone to three sources to protect against this very possibility. The chances that the assassin could have infiltrated all three were very slim indeed. There had to be something else. Something he was missing.

He exhaled heavily. On his own, it wouldn't be such a problem, but the way things had worked out, an innocent was now locked into the struggle. He glanced over his shoulder and saw that she was still sleeping soundly, buried in blankets and dog. He half smiled. Some women—a lot of women, actually—would have been hysterical by now. It said a lot about Claire that she could sleep.

The whole way she'd managed the crisis said a lot about her. She'd followed orders, not in the mindless, stuttering way a lot of civilians would have when faced with a life-or-death situation, but with a cool intelligence edged with fury. Not once had she cried out or whimpered or otherwise expressed terror. When the truck had nearly tipped over, she didn't panic, but simply fought and won control.

A strong woman. No, more than that. Judging by her performance under pressure tonight, she wasn't just strong—she had the instincts of a warrior.

Very sexy.

When the sniper had opened up on them at the inn,

Zane hadn't had time to appreciate the feeling of her body beneath the protective shield of his own. But his subconscious, ever ready to serve the male sex drive, had cataloged details neatly, and he found he could call them up quite clearly now. Her hair, silky and thick against his hand. Her breasts, high and firm, pressed hard into his chest. Her thigh wedged between his, and his between hers. He could recall the fierce anger in her bright blue eyes, and the feel of her small, delicate jaw under his fingers.

Oh, yeah. His organ stirred in its usual conscience-less and indiscriminate bid for attention, and Zane shifted in annoyance.

Bad idea.

As if she agreed with the thought, she rolled over in the back seat. "Damn, it's cold!" she said. "Why don't you turn on the motor and let the heat run for a minute?"

He chuckled at the grouchiness in her voice. "I can do that. Let me step out and check to be sure the exhaust is clear first."

"I'll do it," she said, sitting up. "Nature calls, anyway."

Earlier, Zane had noticed the genteel edges of a Southern drawl, but now, maybe because of her sleepiness, it was thick as honey. It added another plus to the sexy column, and he couldn't quite stop himself from imagining how he'd like to have that honey dripping into his ear under far more intimate circumstances.

She took her dog with her and came back in a few minutes. She let Coach into the back seat, and climbed in the front. Her hair was mussed, sticking up right on top, and impulsively, Zane reached over to smooth it down. She shook his hand off in a wordless rebuff and hunched over the steering column, her hand on the keys. "You think it's dangerous to have the engine sound, Mr. FBI?"

"No. And I'm not the FBI."

"I know what you said. You're some kind of law, though, isn't that a fact?"

He hesitated. "Not in the way you think."

Yawning, she took a brush from her pocket and took out the barrette holding her hair back. It swung free, long and pretty, over her shoulders. Blue sparks leapt between brush and hair. "So why don't you tell me what it really is? Some kind of espionage or something? Is there a terrorist on your tail?"

The more she talked, the more the accent eased, as if she donned a new persona in her waking self. It intrigued him. "Where are you from?"

"I asked you first."

"So you did. And I have to tell you again that you don't really want to know."

"Then I'm not going to answer, either." She slumped against the seat and huddled into her coat. "Lord, I hate being cold."

Zane couldn't help it—he laughed. "Cranky without your coffee, are you?"

She turned her head, and to his surprise, a reluctant smile edged her mouth. "Maybe a little."

He glanced at his watch. "They serve coffee on the ferry, don't they?"

"You aren't going to let me go, are you."

He sobered. "You'd be dead by morning."

She absorbed the information for a long moment. "I hate this," she said at last.

"I'll find a way to make it up to you," he said. "I promise."

"Unless, of course, the bad guy wins, right? Then we're both cooked."

"I'll win," he said.

"Whatever you say." She turned the heater on, full blast. "I need some coffee. We can get on the ferry early."

"Probably a good idea. We'll have a better chance of boarding unobserved."

She paused in the act of putting the vehicle in gear. "I didn't even think about that."

"I did. Trust me, it'll be okay."

Chapter 4

Boarding the ferry proved to be very simple and un-eventful, much to Claire's relief. Her nerves were strained to the breaking point, and her jaw ached from gritting her teeth. She didn't need any more surprises.

To avoid observation, Zane settled behind the back seat with a pile of blankets over him. Coach sat in the passenger seat as he always did. And although Claire felt guilty about bilking the ferry company out of a fare, she purchased her ticket and drove on board as she had dozens of times before.

It was a Sunday morning, only a few days before Christmas, and there were few passengers aboard, es-pecially so early. Anyone else who wanted to get to Seattle or Bainbridge for last-minute shopping would catch the later ferries. Claire recognized most of the handful of other cars in the belly of the boat, and beside her, Zane said approvingly, "No rentals."

Leaving Coach in the car, they climbed the stairs to

the main deck. On the way up, Zane said, "We're on the alert for a woman, very small—probably no more than five-one or -two, barely a hundred pounds."

"Hair? Eyes?"

He lifted a shoulder. "I don't know. Because of…certain aspects of some of the crimes committed, we've been able to figure out her size, but to my knowledge, you're the only one to have spoken to her. Could you make any guesses on age?"

"The sniper is a woman?" Claire asked. "That was her on the phone?"

A nod. "Anything you thought about her might help pull some pieces together."

Claire thought of the voice, petulant and playful on the phone. "I'd almost swear it was a French accent. Fairly sophisticated." She frowned. "Not young, but not old." She lifted her brows. "You know what I pictured? Oh, never mind, it's silly."

He put his hand on her arm. "Wait. Please tell me."

She stopped and turned to face him—and was suddenly slammed with his physical presence for the first time since all the insanity had begun. In her anger and fear, she'd somehow forgotten that he was as gorgeous as a fallen angel.

He stood several steps below her, forcing him to look up, an angle that displayed the light-struck green eyes and exotic cheekbones to full advantage. Claire hated herself for it, but she even thought, for one tiny second, how easy it would be to kiss him. She could simply tilt forward, put her arms around his shoulders and put her mouth against his.

And for the space of a few breaths, it seemed the same thoughts were in his mind. He swayed closer, and his hand on her arm tightened ever so slightly. His gaze flickered down to her mouth, then up to her eyes again, and she saw the liquid stirring in the depths, that unmistakable look of male desire.

Quickly, she lowered her eyes. "I imagined a dark-haired woman with a chignon and a long white neck, in an evening gown with spaghetti straps. Champagne in her hand. Red lipstick." The picture, so complete, amused her and eased the sense of tension she felt next to him. She smiled and raised her head. "See? Silly—"

"I'm going to regret this," he said in a husky voice, then wrapped his hand in the fabric of the front of her coat and tugged, bringing her body into contact with his—

And kissed her.

Caught by surprise, Claire didn't move. With some distant observer portion of her mind, she noted the fact that his mouth was wide and mobile. The lips were firm, but pliant, like warm clay. He smelled of things she couldn't name, things that made her think of starry nights and fires burning against the cold, and—

Her senses overtook reason in a sudden, explosive instant, and with an intensity she didn't even know she possessed, she responded to the insistent, seductive power of his mouth.

Or at least her body responded. The hand that had ached to touch him slid up his chest, over the surprisingly sculpted round of a shoulder, to his carved jaw, and spread itself out over the angles, her fingers against his cheekbone, her palm against his jaw. Her thumb grazed his mouth, and the feel of it moving against her lips and her thumb together sent a charged, deep shock through her middle. Her mouth, which had wanted last night to taste his lips, opened, and invited a silky tongue into its cavern, where she could tease it, flutter and slide her own tongue against it.

She felt his free hand light on the back of her neck and urge her closer, tilting her head to give deeper access. A hard ache burst in her chest, pounding so hard it nearly hurt, but she didn't pull away or protest. She heard the tiny warning voice cry out that she was a fool, that this was a mistake, but the draw, the pleasure of that mouth was so deep she simply couldn't imagine why she would quit.

He turned his head infinitesimally and sucked the tip of her thumb into their mouths, and Claire honestly buckled at the fierceness of her response. He seemed to anticipate the problem and simply shifted her sideways against the wall, then lifted his head to look at her.

Claire, stunned by her response, simply stared up at him, seeing the glaze of passion on his face. Something hard flickered over his eyes and he pulled back a little. "Classic response to danger," he said roughly. "Sex to affirm life."

Stung, she shoved at his chest. "Indulge it with someone else, bud."

He reached for her arm, but Claire saw it in time and ducked away. Her face flamed with humiliation—how could she have let herself go like that? Hadn't she learned anything from watching her mother all these years?

At the top of the steps, she halted and pressed her back against the wall. In a hard voice, she said, "You're the one she wants to kill. You go first."

His mouth—still shiny with her kiss, she noticed with despair—quirked a tiny bit. "My pleasure, ma'am," he drawled, and tipped an imaginary Stetson.

Laboriously, he limped up the stairs past her, taking one step, then dragging the broken leg behind him. No matter how close she squeezed against the wall, his body brushed hers, shoulder to thigh, and she was enveloped in that scent of starry nights.

She closed her eyes and held her breath till he passed, thinking darkly that it would solve a lot of problems if he just got shot as he entered the main room upstairs.

He didn't, of course. He paused for a moment, and she saw him looking around, then he gestured toward her. "C'mon, grumpy," he said. "Let's get you some caffeine before you draw and quarter me."

"Very funny." Desperate to escape him for a moment, she stopped at the door to the rest room. "I'll join you in a minute. Get me a latte and a Danish, will you?"

Without waiting for his reply, she ducked into the ladies' room and rushed to the sink. She turned on the water and washed her hands. In the mirror, her reflection showed a pinched expression. "What are you doing, Claire?" she said aloud.

Between herself and the mirror, a memory rose. She would not have been able to put a year to the image, but she saw the world in slightly larger focus. Her mother, giggling like a little kid, as a big, dark man buried her in the couch, kissing her. To her shame, Claire saw the man lift her mother's pink nylon uniform and pull off her panties. Then they were doing something else, and the scared little girl protested, running into the room to pound on the man's back, screaming for him to stop.

Embarrassed, they'd scrambled up, readjusting their clothes, and Larissa pulled Claire into her lap. "It's okay, sweetie," she said. "It's just sex. It feels good and you don't have to be afraid for me. But it's not really something for a little girl to be watching."

That had been the first time. Over the years, there had been many others. Her mother was ruled by sex, by her need for a man in her life all the time, and she'd been sexy enough to assure herself of a steady supply.

Claire thought of the strange, deep pulse in her when Zane kissed her. It had been nearly violent in its force. Was that what her mother had felt? What if Claire, after all these years of thinking she was above all that, discovered she had the same wild nature as her mother?

"No," she said. No. The difference between civilization and anarchy was that while humans couldn't avoid feeling things, they could make rational decisions not to act on them. Fate had given her a test by throwing one of the most delectable men she'd ever seen right in her path. Not only that, it appeared she would be trapped with him for a least a day or two.

A test. She intended to pass it.

She found Zane at a booth by the windows. Just as she settled, the ferry began to move through the misty, snowy predawn. Along the edge of the eastern horizon, a serrated line of faint light edged over the mountains.

He had purchased large lattes and big shiny apples and Danishes in cellophane, and passed her cup over. "I figured you liked it sweet," he said, also pushing over a stack of sugar packets.

"Thank you," she said, and was pleased at the cool politeness in her voice. She could do this.

They ate in silence. Claire gazed out at the beloved view and wondered when she would come back this way. If she ever would.

But the truth was, coffee cleared her head, and the

food didn't hurt, either. She glanced at the man across the table, and noticed the skin over his cheekbones was stretched taut. "You must be exhausted," she said.

He rubbed his face, as if to wipe away the evidence. "I'll be all right."

"Will you?" She had a vested interest, after all. "How much sleep have you really had in the past seventy-two hours?"

A frown tugged the artful, dark brows. "Three, maybe four hours. And I dozed on the planes, here and there."

"Those razor-sharp reflexes have to be fairly rusty by now."

"Yeah, maybe."

Claire laced her fingers around her cup. "I have an idea. Let's get off at Bainbridge Island and find some little town with a hole-in-the-wall motel where you can sleep."

"So you can ditch me and get yourself killed? I think not."

She rolled her eyes. "I'm not stupid. I'm not happy, you understand, but I'm in no hurry to get myself shot, either. And since my only chance of survival looks to be one ragged-at-the-edges, broken-legged, exhausted Indian, I'd just as soon he got some rest."

His grin was quick and gorgeous. "I guess it makes a certain amount of sense when you put it like that." He narrowed his eyes in thought. "But I'm not sure an island is our best chance of survival."

"We'll get off there, but there's a bridge off the island to the west. A zillion little towns, and it's close by the reservation, so you won't stand out any."

"You've got it all worked out."

"Lot of practice," she said briskly, and shifted her gaze to the gradually lightening view.

"A lot of practice running away with a burned-out...no, wait." He grinned. "A 'ragged-at-the-edges, broken-legged, exhausted Indian'?"

He imitated her faint drawl perfectly, and Claire couldn't help but smile ruefully. "You do that pretty well, Mr. Hunter. You have no idea how many hours I've practiced getting rid of that drawl, and there you are, mocking me with it."

He winked. "Good ear, eh?"

"Not bad."

"I like the accent," he said. "You oughta keep it."

She shrugged. "I'm stuck with it." She shrugged. "Trust me, it really isn't all that charming. You wouldn't believe how many people think you're dense if you have a Southern accent. They'll slow down their speech—" she exaggerated the process "—till... they're...speaking...like...this. And they'll start picking one-syllable words instead of three. It's insulting." She sipped her coffee. "Thing I hate the most, though? Lots of people think you're just naturally a born racist, too, like you have hidden Confederate flags tattooed on you somewhere."

"You mean you don't? Not even a little one, maybe—" he wiggled his eyebrows "—on a breast or something?"

"Not even there."

"Too bad."

"Not that you'd see it, anyway."

A teasing sultriness darkened his bright eyes. "If I asked very, very nicely?"

Flirtation she could handle. With a sleepy gaze of her own, she said, "You wish."

He grinned. "You're something, Claire Franklin. I don't think I've met a woman like you before."

"Never will again, either."

"I'm sure." He leaned back, eyeing the view. "I get the same thing from some people. Slow talk, simple words." He shot her a wicked glance. "Everybody knows how bad the reservation schools are, you know. Pitiful. Poor, neglected noble Indians."

"Ah."

"But like you, I hate something else more—people who think you've got some line to the Great Spirit or some other crap. Got a story with turtles or talking antelopes for every occasion."

"You mean you don't?" Claire replied, tongue-in-cheek.

"Well—" he winked. "I might have a spider story or two. But I've had communication problems with the Big Guy for a while now."

There was the faintest hint of despair in the words. Claire bit her lip to keep from asking why. She didn't want to know. She didn't want to like him, and heaven help her, that was just what she was starting to do. "I know the feeling," she said lightly. "I've got a real beef to pick about this sniper-spy thing I've got going on." Before he could reply, she stood up. "We'd best get back to the car. We're almost there."

The sun had come up by the time they disembarked at Bainbridge, but the only indication was a lighter sky. The snow had stopped, but the skies remained gray and heavy as Claire wound around the island and crossed the bridge to the western mainland. Next to her, Zane blinked hard and shifted regularly, obviously trying to stay awake.

"I can handle this part," she said. "Why don't you grab a pillow and catch a few winks?"

"It's not—"

She gave him a look. "It's easy. I'll keep driving till I find some cozy little hole-in-the-wall, and then I'll wake you. Simple."

"I'll just doze a little." He reached back for the pillow, nested it against the door, and in a minute flat, was literally snoring. Claire chuckled. Good that he had a flaw in there somewhere.

She drove southwest through thick forest and tiny towns, all decorated for the season with red bows and bells hung from the lampposts. With the newly fallen snow, it all looked incredibly serene and Christmasy, and Claire thought of her perfectly decorated tree drying out with no one to admire it.

Irrelevant, she told herself. The house would be fine. There were no guests to be disappointed. As timing for a kidnapping went, this was about the best she could hope for.

The gas gauge read dangerously low, and Claire resolved to stop in the next small town, both for gas and sleep. Her own eyes were grainy, and her neck was tight from tension.

In the next small town, she stopped at a convenience store for gas. Zane did not awaken. She filled the tank, bought an assortment of snack foods—oranges out of a refrigerated case, packages of cracker sandwiches, chocolate, candy canes, bottles of juice—and he still had not awakened.

Which left the choice of lodgings up to her. Away from the main road, she stumbled over the Swiss Village Motel, a collection of tiny A-frame units with false fronts depicting painted Heidis and Hans cheerily smil-

ing from the fake upper stories. Plastic red geraniums
bloomed from window boxes. The sign showed a va-
cancy, and she pulled up in front.

Zane started awake. "Where are we?"

"Fifty miles from nothing," Claire said, picking up
her purse. "I'm going to go register."

"Use a fake name," he said. "And don't put down
the right numerals for your license plate." He rubbed
his face. "Better yet, let me do it. I have a little more
practice."

"Okay."

He came back in a minute with a key attached to a
miniature version of the A-frames. "This is almost ter-
minally cute," he said dryly, and pointed the way to
the third chalet from the end. "Park in the back."

The room was small and warm. Standard motel-issue
furniture was enlivened by cheerful blue-and-yellow
bedspreads and a good clean carpet. The painting over
the two double beds rendered the Alps in a nearly competent manner. Zane locked the door behind them,
drew the drapes and gestured toward the beds. "Do
you have a preference?"

Claire shook her head. It suddenly seemed very intimate to be here with a man she hadn't known existed
twenty-four hours ago. It also seemed odd that she
trusted him. Especially since he was not only a
stranger, but a big sexy man with a wicked glint in his
eye and a kiss that said he'd sinned often, and with
great gusto.

She stood by the door, made awkward by the sudden
awareness of the situation. Keeping her hands wedged
deeply in her pockets, she watched Coach pad around
the room, his nose to the floor, following the serpentine
path of some exotic scent, so that she wouldn't have

to look at Zane taking off his coat. His hat. His shoes. The rubber band that held his thick, heavy black hair away from his face.

Please don't let him take off his shirt!

His long-fingered, graceful hands went to the buttons, and Claire bolted for the bathroom. "I'm going to take a shower," she said without looking at him. "Do you mind?"

"Not at all." Wearily, he stripped off the shirt and let if fall to the floor, completely oblivious to Claire's greedy, sidelong glances.

One: a flash of buttery-looking skin, smooth and brown.

Another: sinews across powerful shoulders and a completely hairless chest.

Another: arms lean but muscular.

One more: a belly as flat as a mesa.

Claire was staring. At a long lock of black hair lying in perfect grace across his collarbone. At the dark, flat nipples. At the dip of his waist. Her ears got hot and she told herself to move, to get on with it, get out of here, before she did something stupid. Before the completely exhausted man in the bed realized that she was mooning at him with sex in her eyes, that they were together in a small room and had no place to go until they got some rest.

A brutal memory of her mother crossed her imagination. Larissa, not more than thirty, swaying into the living room with lust making her pretty, worn face look like a caricature. Claire was fourteen, and appalled that her mother would wear a satin blouse—trashy enough all by itself—with no bra underneath, her nipples sticking out as she gazed at the man who slept in the chair. Awful.

With a shudder, Claire rushed into the bathroom and slammed the door, leaning against it as if there were demons in pursuit. Then, abruptly, she turned on the shower, hot. She tore off her coat and let it fall on the floor, kicked off her shoes, shucked her blouse and her jeans and her underpants and bra. Steam hid her reflection in the mirror, and she got into the shower, realizing there were tears on her face. Tears.

She never cried, and now she'd done it twice in twenty-four hours. But then, it had been one hell of a day. Ripped away from her home. Fleeing from a sniper. Stuck with a man who brought out every lustful impulse she'd denied for years.

She put her face under the spray and pretended she wasn't weeping. Pretended, most of all, that she was not her mother's daughter.

Zane was nearly asleep when he heard Coach whining. Very low, very sad. He wondered if the dog needed to go outside. The shower was running, which left Zane to do the duty. He'd left his jeans on, much as he hated to, out of deference to his obviously nervous roommate, and now he tossed off the covers, pulled a blanket around him and hobbled toward the door. "C'mon, Coach," he said, "I'll take you."

The shepherd shifted, foot to foot, but he didn't move, only glanced back to the closed bathroom door, ears cocked. He whined again, that most mournful of sad and lonely sounds.

Zane had forgotten how perfectly expressive dogs could be, and it was a little shock to realize how far removed he was from the man he'd once been. The recognition was a small, swift knife thrust, there and gone before he could fully register it. "It's all right, guy,'' he said, limping around the bed. Laboriously, he lowered himself to the floor, his cast stuck out in front of him, and rubbed the dog's ears. ''She'll be out in a little while.''

Coach licked his wrist and stood up, ready to go in the bathroom just as soon as someone opened the door for him. He looked at the handle, then back at Zane as if to say, hurry up.

Zane shook his head. ''Can't do it, man.'' He had to admit the idea had appeal. It was hard not to imagine her wet and slippery with soap, that perfect rear end bare and—

Coach barked, once, sharply, as if he'd heard Zane's thoughts.

He grinned. ''Sorry. You gotta admit she's a pretty sexy little thing, though. You know how it is.''

But the dog would not be soothed. He whined, and even bent over and nudged Zane's hand with his cold, wet nose, as if to get him up and open the damned door. ''What's wrong with you?'' Zane asked, puzzled.

And then he heard it. Very faint weeping mixed in with the sound of the shower.

He swore. He supposed she deserved a good, cleansing cry, but he couldn't help thinking of her forlorn weeping over the Christmas tree, and her pleasure in getting it right. He thought of the big, rambling inn, so warm and filled with good smells and the genuine mark of a homemaker in every detail, thought of her soup and excellent coffee and the thick towels he'd enjoyed after his shower there.

Then he took in the packages of cheese and crackers, the bag of oranges, the bottles of juice that she'd set on the dresser.

"Damn," he said aloud, and struggled to pull himself to his feet. "You're right, Coach, she needs you."

Once he was stabilized, he knocked on the door sharply. "Claire!"

"I'll be done in a minute."

"Your dog wants in right now. I'm just going to open the door and let him in, okay?"

"Sure."

He turned the handle. Locked. Good for her. "Uh, Claire? You're going to have to do it. It's locked." As if to add his voice, Coach barked again. Loudly.

"Just a minute."

He stepped back, meaning to limp away, turn his head and give her some privacy, but he backed into the nightstand and overbalanced in the blasted cast. He was struggling to catch the lamp and keep himself balanced when she opened the door. A wave of soap-scented steam wafted out, and he caught a glimpse of a bare, wet shoulder and a slice of wet hair before she closed the door again.

His body stirred at the sight. Zane adjusted his jeans to accommodate his sudden arousal, and scowled. If it weren't for hormones, a man could live a lot more dignified kind of life. To distract himself, he opened some of the cheese and crackers and a bottle of juice. He was starving. He was exhausted.

And sick to death of this life.

The thought shocked him, but it barely registered before the bathroom door opened and Claire came out. She'd put her clothes back on and combed her hair back from her face, but her feet were bare. They were small, delicate white feet, to match the rest of her small, delicate body, and he noticed her toenails were painted the softest imaginable shade of shell pink.

"You okay?" he asked.

A nod, but the turquoise eyes were suspiciously bright, and he thought he glimpsed, for the most fleeting of moments, a flash of hunger in them. She quickly controlled it.

Unceremoniously, she dumped her coat and shoes on the floor by the bed, threw back the covers and climbed in. "I'm going to sleep now," she announced.

"Take off your jeans, honey," Zane said gently. "Slip them off under the covers. I was trying to sleep in mine, and it was miserable."

"I'm one step ahead of you," she said, and wiggled out of them. They fell off on the other side of the bed. "Turn around now."

He obliged but noticed he could see her in the mirror just fine. She slid her bra straps off her arms and tugged the garment out of her left sleeve. He watched curiously to see what sort of underwear she chose. If asked, he would have guessed she wore utilitarian cotton bras and panties.

He would have been wrong. The slip of fabric emerging from her sleeve was a rich blue-green color. And he thought it was velvet. "Neat trick," he said wickedly.

She caught his gaze in the mirror, and for a moment, he thought with a little thrill that she was going to throw the only weapon handy squarely at his head. He even had a second to imagine the warmth her breasts had lent the fabric before she realized it would be a tactical error and threw it on top of her jeans. With a huff, she settled on the pillows, then patted the place beside her. "Come on, baby," she said to her dog. "You have to protect me from evil forces."

He chuckled, then popped the last bite of cracker

into his mouth. Suddenly worried that she might be concocting an elaborate ruse, he said abruptly, "Where are the keys to the truck?"

"You still don't trust me after all this?" she asked.

"It's not about trust. It's about keeping you out of harm's way."

"Right." She rolled her eyes but reached over the edge of the bed, pulled the ring of keys from her coat pocket and tossed them to him. "Good night, Zane."

He caught them midair and turned off the lights on the way to the bed. "I can't get in and out of my jeans under the covers," he said. "So I'm warning you now I'm about to pull them off."

"I'll try to resist temptation," she said dryly.

"Good. I'm wearing my cupid boxers, and a guy hates to get caught in something so sentimental."

"I'm still resisting."

He skimmed the jeans down. "They're pink and white."

"Liar."

It was his turn to laugh. "You're right. They're plain green stripes."

She made a noise of exasperation as he climbed into the bed, but she still didn't turn over, much to his disappointment. "What makes you think I have the faintest interest in your underwear?"

The drawl was coming back now, deepening with each word as her guard dropped. "Wishful thinking, I guess." He punched the pillow and tried to get comfortable. The heavy drapes sealed out even the faintest bit of light and he closed his eyes, sure it would be easy to sleep.

It wasn't. He turned. Then turned again. Readjusted the pillows. On the bed next to him, Claire seemed to be going through the same motions. He heard her sigh heavily.

"Anything I can do?" he asked, adding a perfect note of wickedness.

"I hate to sleep away from home," she admitted. "You'd think I'd be used to it. I spent seven years opening up new hotels for a chain, and I bet I didn't sleep in the same bed more than two months running in all that time."

"I know how that is."

"I bet you do, Mr. Secret Agent Man. But instead of Boise and Albuquerque and Tampa, I bet you were in Brussels and Moscow and London."

"Sometimes."

"I've never traveled out of the country," she said after a minute. "What's it like?"

Her voice eased him, with its slightly husky under-note and softened vowels. The strain in his shoulders began to leak out slowly. To please her, he said, "It's great."

"What's your favorite city?"

He ran through the possibilities. The old streets of Munich. The famed pigeons in Rome. The women, so exotic and plentiful and gorgeous, in Rio. "A lot of them are beautiful," he said slowly. "But they're all crowded and noisy and polluted on one level or another. I don't like cities much."

"Really? I don't, either. I was raised in a little town, though. Were you?"

"Very small." A clear, strong memory of it moved against the dark screen of his eyelids. "Up in the mountains, little tiny place. My dad wasn't crazy about cities, either. My mom came from Chicago, but she never looked back once she met my father."

"Must be your mom who gave you the green eyes, then." Her voice was slowing, slowing.

"Yep. She was rushing to L.A. for some film thing when she was in college, and had a wreck with a pickup truck. My dad was a cop, and he was there, holding her hand while they cut her out."

"How awful! Was she badly hurt?"

"She lost a leg, but she always says it was the luckiest thing that ever happened to her. My dad was at that hospital every day, bringing her food and flowers. By the time she got well, he talked her into getting married."

"That's a very romantic story. How could you leave people like that and go around the world?"

It struck him as an odd question, but he answered it honestly. "It's a long story." He shrugged in the darkness. "My dad was gone by the time I left. He died when I was ten."

"Oh. I'm sorry. What happened?"

Zane sighed. "Got shot in a domestic violence call. Pretty senseless."

"It must have broken your mother's heart."

"Pretty much." He shifted once again, thinking of the way she had changed after that. For a year or so, it seemed all the light left her. Her hair got drab and she never cared about the way she looked. "It was pretty hard on her, but she got religion and now she's okay."

She chuckled. "Got religion?"

"Yep. Joined the Evergreen First Evangelical Church, and things got better—at least for her—right away."

"You didn't like church?"

He had to think about that. As a boy, it had driven

him crazy to have to go three times a week: Sunday mornings, Sunday evenings and Wednesday prayer meetings and Bible studies. It bored him to death.

But in more recent years, he'd found himself sometimes remembering the dusty, churchy smell and the look of the sanctuary, so warm and welcoming, after dark. "It was okay. I hated the Bible study. She let me off the hook on that when I was sixteen or so." He paused, remembering Christmas Eve with candles in hand and carols rising into the soft, warm dark. "I liked the singing."

"You don't strike me as a man who likes to sing, somehow."

A strange but welcome peace stole through him and he settled more luxuriously into the pillow. "I did," he said, and was overtaken by a yawn. "Don't do it anymore."

"Hmmm." She, too, seemed wound down.

"Sleep well," he said quietly, but doubted she even heard him. Then sleep swallowed him, too.

Chapter 5

In the gathering evening, Simone Chevalier, known to the world only as the Ghost, tapped the keys of her computer keyboard quickly. A tiny, elegant lamp burned on the desk behind her small but extremely powerful laptop, and the light shone like a ruby in her wine, illuminating the crystal ashtray and her slim brown cigarette. Beyond her high window, lights sparkled over Puget Sound, and she could make out a line of rush-hour traffic along a major artery from the city.

But here, in the lush suite, there was only silence. Her face was utterly still and composed as she tracked leads—first the obvious, and not likely used, passport names Hunter had assembled in France. Nothing. She had not expected him to make such a large error. If he were that stupid, this game would never have begun. Still, she'd paid enormous sums for the names, and it would not do to leave the detail unchecked.

Next, she typed in his real name. Nothing. Again, expected.

She rolled her shoulders and took a long breath. There was no hurry. The first encounter had gone to Hunter. The next would go to Simone. She did not often fail, and never if she was fully prepared.

Except when Zane Hunter was involved.

The thought carried with it a tense frustration. Twice now he'd slipped through her net. And twice more, he'd outthought her and prevented assassinations that were worth millions. In her fury last spring, she'd been sloppy.

No, a stubborn voice argued. Not sloppy. How could she know Hunter would drink too much wine and turn over his keys to his friend?

She should have. Her research had been thin. Too thin.

That mistake was not one she would make again. She knew him better now than his mother did. She could think as he thought. Walk as he walked. Dream his dreams.

But now a second element had been introduced, the element that had saved Hunter at the inn: Claire Franklin.

It was tempting to dismiss her as a homemaker type, trembling in her pumps and pearls when bullets shattered the peace of her world. The Ghost had believed her to be a helpless mass of despised, trembling female flesh, but that had proved to be a mistake. Without Franklin, Hunter could never have escaped. The Ghost had counted on that one small, important fact: Hunter could not drive with that cast.

She tapped numbers into a form on the screen. The mistake had cost her, but the game was still in her court. After a long day of sleep, she was ready to tackle the next steps.

A bleeping cursor, showing a clock face with time elapsing, flashed on the screen. Simone settled back, her cigarette between deceptively delicate fingers, and inhaled, waiting. Suddenly, the cursor disappeared and a black screen came up. In it, Simone could see herself in a somewhat—she smiled—ghostly fashion, her cropped dark hair and long neck a single line. She smoked, and at last a database, highly secret and supposedly impossible to hack, opened. She typed in the name, retrieved a social security number and moved to a second screen.

A satisfying list scrolled down the monitor—Claire Franklin's paper history on the planet. There were employers, bank accounts, transactions of virtually every imaginable sort, addresses and telephone numbers, high school and college transcripts. The Ghost highlighted each one in turn, at first simply scrolling through, getting a feel for the woman who had changed this equation.

She'd started work young, at Geena's Café in Henderson, Arkansas, where she'd made $2.10 an hour plus tips, thirty hours a week when she was thirteen. It seemed a lot of work for a young girl. Simone doubted it was even legal, but Claire Franklin had kept the job till she left for college at seventeen. Also early.

Simone tapped the tip of her finger against her lower lip as Claire Franklin's history emerged. Hardworking. Underprivileged, as the Americans said. "Poor," they called it in the Paris slums where she'd grown up. Simone smoked and clicked the mouse.

College had been a struggle. Scholarships and loans and, even then, late payments on the tuition some semesters. Through the cloud of blue smoke, Simone narrowed her eyes and clicked on a new screen. Various kinds of purchases, everything from magazines and books to cars, insurance, a condo in Michigan two years after college, bank accounts that showed the woman could live on a shoestring. She'd saved an impressive amount of money in five years, enough to couple with the sale of the condo to buy the inn.

It took hours, but Simone finally found a critical piece of information: a credit card in Lackey, Washington, yesterday morning.

She smiled and picked up the phone. "I would like my car brought up, please."

Zane awakened disoriented. A dark room. Too warm. His cast was weighted by a pile of blankets, his hair tangled around his neck. Outside, the sound of a heavy rain. No traffic noises. No birds.

The low, rumbling groan of a sleeping dog snapped things into focus. The motel in western Washington, with the pretty innkeeper and her dog. He sat up abruptly and listened, wondering what had awakened him.

Maybe the rain. It pounded overhead like a warning of Armageddon, and he got up to peer through the drapes. A family rushed from one of the other cottages to a car, the newspapers over their heads soaked before they ran two feet. A little girl squealed and jumped in a puddle with her rainboots.

The snow was gone, and ran water down the slight slope of the street beyond in a rush. Judging by the light, it was late afternoon.

A slight rustle of covers reminded him that he was barely dressed, and he turned to get his jeans from the bottom of the bed. Claire had not awakened. In the small bar of light from the crack in the drapes, he could see she was still very much asleep, the pillows tucked close to her chest, the honey-colored hair scattered over her face. Even in sleep, her expression was guarded, her head tucked down as if she were hiding. It plucked at him, somewhere deep.

It would be so easy to slip under the covers with her, slide into the island of warmth made by her body and circle her with himself. Nestle close and let her breasts flow against his chest, coax a thigh between hers, cup the pretty bottom in his hands. He'd like kissing her awake. Mouth and throat and breasts, exposed just a half inch of flesh at a time as he unbuttoned her shirt.

As if she felt his scrutiny, she shifted, and Zane hastily struggled into his jeans, cursing the cast once again. He was ready for the damned thing to come off—now. He tugged his shirt on, which was beginning to smell a little stale, and he grimaced. They needed supplies. Mentally, he made a list—some new clothes, toothbrushes, hot coffee and a decent meal.

An itch prickled along his casted knee. He added a hacksaw to the list.

And a plan. He'd been so fried yesterday that coherent thought had been beyond him, but a solid seven hours' sleep had cleared the jet lag, and he felt a sense of urgency. The Ghost would not luck across them. They'd left no trail.

But Zane had to end this, on his own terms, and to do that, he would have to lure the assassin out.

One step at a time. He couldn't do a damned thing in the cast. It came off first. Then he'd figure out what to do with Claire, and where to stage the showdown.

Dressed, he made his way to the bathroom, resolving

he'd take a thorough shower when he got the cast off. He washed his face and combed his hair, adding shampoo to the growing list of things they needed. There had been a little café and drugstore on the other side of the office—they'd have coffee and toiletries between them. The hacksaw presented a little more of a problem.

Frowning, he came out into the dark room, and light from the bathroom illuminated the bed nearest the door. Although she still hugged the pillows, Claire had pushed the covers away in the too-warm room. He halted, his hand on the light switch, unable to force himself to click it off right away.

The shirt was long sleeved and covered her decently—except it had ridden up in back a little, just enough to reveal a pair of rich blue-green panties made of the same soft fabric as the bra on the floor. Definitely velvet, he decided, and his mouth went dry. The elastic on the panties curved in an upward circle, revealing the bare lower half of a perfectly formed buttock, the flesh as creamy and supple as doeskin. He could not help imagining the way the velvet and skin would feel in combination. Once, twice, three times, he saw himself move, walking across the small space between them, bending over her, reaching out a hand to explore that beautiful leg and bottom. He wondered how she would respond. If it would arouse her or make her angry.

Or both. He thought of the heat of her mouth when he kissed her on the stairs of the ferry, remembered the erotic play of her tongue against his own, and the dazed, hungry look in her eyes when he let her go— and the anger in her afterward.

She'd be angry. But if he kissed her, she wouldn't protest for long. They could spend the evening having what he suspected would be some pretty outrageous sex. The chemistry between them was powerful, and danger gave it an added edge—oh, yeah. Very good sex, to break his long celibacy.

He almost took that first step, felt the electric impulse hit his uncasted knee, and a bolt of memory halted him. A forlorn child-woman weeping in an empty room with a tawdry Christmas tree.

When the hell had he lost his humanity? She might seem tough, and he had no doubt at all that she could be seduced, but that didn't mean it was right.

And then, with a cold insight, he realized he'd babbled on about his family and his life, revealing more of himself to her in a single hour than he'd let anyone know in fifteen years. He also realized, with a narrowing of his eyes, that he had no idea who she was, or where she was from.

Losing it, a voice said in his mind. Letting down his guard was a sure way to get himself killed.

Abruptly, he slammed the light off. In the darkness, he scrawled a note on hotel stationery and propped it against the mirror.

The rain outside hit him with cold, cleansing fingers. And he stood in it for a moment, allowing it to punish him for his lapse. When he'd chosen this life, he'd chosen to leave behind the man who could tell his life to a woman in the darkness. If he got soft now, the Ghost would pick off both him and an innocent who'd been dragged into the situation unwillingly, like a child stepping on ants.

Zane couldn't let that happen. He'd long ago made his peace with death. Every time he took an assignment, he spun the barrel in a cosmic game of Russian roulette. In the past four or five years, he hadn't even really had that much to lose.

But he thought of the warm, cheery inn, so welcoming and rich, and knew Claire had a lot to lose. She deserved to die an old grandmother, rocking babies in her lap.

Whatever happened to him, however the game went down between Zane and the Ghost, Zane would not allow Claire to be sacrificed. And to keep himself aloof enough to safeguard his instincts, he could not allow a physical liaison to develop. His fatal weakness had always been the warm body of a woman, the murmur of her laughter in his ear. He got soft over them. Wanted to please them and take care of them.

This time, that would be a mistake fatal to both of them.

Whatever it took, he had to stay aloof.

Claire surfaced slowly, aware of someone calling her name. It seemed to take a million years to decide where it was coming from. Who could be calling her? She lived alone. She made her own hours.

Persistently, it came again, and finally the scent of coffee penetrated her sleep-drugged brain. She opened one eye.

To see a face she thought she had imagined, with blades of cheekbones and the mouth of a fallen god, and sex in the dark green eyes. She blinked slowly, feeling a wave of sensual yearning roll down her spine.

"Honey, if you lie there and look at me that way, I will not be responsible for my actions." He straightened. "C'mon. Rise and shine. I need your help."

Oh, God.

It all came back to her. The Christmas tree. Zane. The bullets. The ferry—

And that kiss. In her vulnerable in-between state, it was as immediate as if it still lived, his strong mouth and hands on her, his—

She closed her eyes, covering her face. "Give me a minute," she croaked.

The sound of his uneven gait told her he'd moved away. Claire became aware of the chill on her legs and bottom, and reached for the blanket to pull over herself. When she was covered, she tossed her hair out of her eyes, and said, "You have coffee?"

Wordless, smileless, he handed her a paper cup, then went back to the task at hand, unlacing the cut in his jeans to expose the cast. It was oddly clean of the scribblings and doodles casts usually seemed to sport. "What are you doing?"

He lifted a hacksaw. "I'm going to cut this off."

"Is that wise?"

"Hell of a lot wiser than leaving it on." He looked at her, and Claire saw a coldness she had not glimpsed before. It sent a ripple of worry down her spine. Maybe she hadn't believed any of this was real, but that determined, hard expression told her how serious it all was. "If I get it off, I can work on getting the strength back."

She nodded and sipped the hot, sweet coffee, watching as he propped the leg on the bed and got to work. Slowly, her brain came to life and she scrambled, modestly under the covers, into her jeans.

"I brought you some clothes," he said without looking up. "In that bag over there. I got them a little bigger than I thought you'd be, just in case."

"Thank you." Claire opened the bag and found a

blue T-shirt and pair of jeans, even—she couldn't help a faint heat coming to her cheeks—underwear. Beneath them was a package of T-shirts she assumed were for him. "That was thoughtful."

A nod, distant and aloof. "Once you get dressed, I could use some help."

"No problem." Puzzled by his change in attitude, she scurried into the bathroom, pleased to be able to take off the rumpled flannel shirt she'd been wearing for thirty-six hours and put on something fresh. The jeans fit so perfectly, she suspected he'd checked the size on the pair she'd left on the floor. The shirt was pretty, a touristy thing with a Douglas fir emblazoned on the front and a scoop neck and long sleeves. Soft cotton that felt very good. It was a little big, but not so bad she couldn't live with it.

Looking at herself in the mirror, she saw that the color brought out the deepest blues in her eyes and lent her makeup-less face a hint of color. "Ugh," she said to her reflection, wishing for at least a little mascara or something. With a shrug, she scrubbed her face, tugged up the slipping side of the T-shirt and went out to help Zane.

He'd sawed through most of the thigh and knee, all the way down to the soft cloth liner. A pile of plaster shavings littered the bed below him. "I can't reach the calf," he said. "Will you do the honors?"

"Sure." She put her coffee aside and took the saw, then frowned as she considered the logistics. "Maybe it would be easiest if I pull a chair over and you put your foot in my lap."

"Whatever."

She grinned. "Who's grumpy now, grumpy?"

He scowled. "I'm sick of this thing. It's been on six months."

Claire dragged a chair from in front of the vanity, and he swung his leg into her lap. She had to shift sideways to get the proper angle. "So how'd you do it, Mr. CIA?" she asked casually as she started to saw. "The bad guys catch you in an alley or something?"

"Something like that."

Since he seemed disinclined to talk, she concentrated on the task. It wasn't hard, but the T-shirt slid off her shoulder a couple of times and she had to stop to tug it up.

The second time, she sighed. "I need a safety pin, I think."

"Guess I got it a little too big, huh?"

She glanced up. "It's okay. I have narrow shoulders. My mama always said I'd be glad later because it would make me look smaller if I got fat." She chuckled. "In the meantime, I have to pin a lot of things."

He grunted in reply.

"Almost there." Claire sawed carefully as the blade went deeper, afraid she would cut him. In the silence, she became aware that his toe was millimeters away from her right nipple, and the instant she realized it, the tip hardened, as if stretching toward it. Heat burned in her ears, and she sawed more fiercely, thankful for a good bra that hid her reaction. Or at least she hoped it had.

Just as she sawed through the last bit of cast, the T-shirt fell off her shoulder again, and exasperated, she left it while she finished, then tugged it up and put the saw aside. "Okay, we're done. How do you want to do this?"

He swung the foot back to the bed. "You grab that

end, and I'll grab this, and we'll crack it open. Ready?''

She slid her fingers into the crevice she'd sawed into the plaster. "Ready."

"Pull."

The cast gave way with a crack, leaving a gauzy underdressing. "Hang on," Claire said. "I saw a sewing kit in the bathroom. There were scissors in there." She fetched it, gave him the scissors, then took a moment to pin the T-shirt to her bra straps. "Much better."

One wicked eyebrow flew up, as if he couldn't resist. "That's a matter of opinion."

She chuckled, a little relieved that he had teased her. Then she fell on her knees to help remove the remnants of plaster and gauze and cottony packing from the injured leg. He cut through the lowest layer, and finally, the bare leg was revealed. "Thank God," Zane said emphatically, rubbing his knee. "I've wanted to scratch that spot for months."

Sobered, Claire rocked back on her heels. The leg had been badly mangled, judging by the scars in three places. Raw stitch marks showed where parts had been sewn back together, and other purplish places showed the impact of whatever had hit him.

"Not too pretty, is it?"

"No." Wordlessly, she rose and took the ice container into the bathroom. She filled it with hot water, then carried a bar of soap, a washcloth and a pile of towels back with her. She knelt beside him and put the towels beneath his leg.

"Claire, you don't have to do that. I can take care of it."

"I don't mind. You won't be able to reach it as well

as I can.'' Dipping the rag into the water, she soaped
it up and began to methodically wash away the dead
skin and bits of cotton. She started with his foot, high-
arched and as sinewy as his hands, soaping and rinsing
and drying a section at a time. "What really happened?'' she asked quietly.

"The bad guys got me.''

His voice held a rough undernote, and Claire looked
up. His face was shuttered. "I know that much.'' She
turned back to her task, dipping the washcloth in the
hot water again.

"I don't want to talk about it. Tell me about yourself, Claire,'' he said.

She lifted a shoulder. "Nothing to tell, really.''

"Where's your family?''

"I don't have any.''

"None?''

She took a breath and shook her hair from her face.
This was the point when she usually made something
up. A car accident. Foster homes. Dead soldier fathers
and heartbroken mothers. Anything but the truth.

This time, she couldn't bring up a lie that sounded
plausible. "I probably have some grandparents somewhere, but I've never known them, and my mama died
when I was eighteen.''

"I'm sorry.''

"Don't be.'' She washed his knee and the curved
stitch marks, carefully looking at his leg instead of his
face. "I'm not.''

A ripple of stillness met her words, and she looked
up defensively. He met her gaze evenly. "I don't believe that.''

She shrugged. "Believe what you want.'' She bent
over to get the ice bucket. "I'll be right back.''

* * *

Zane let out his breath when she left the room and tried to think of something to distract himself. The woman was torturing him. He had to get her to a safe house, someplace far away from him. Safe from him.

The shirt had been a big mistake. All by itself, it would have been a bad choice. The color made her eyes almost neon blue, as compelling as a siren song, and the soft fabric draped over her slim form with exactitude, showing every swell and dip of her upper body.

But the neckline was pure torture, falling artlessly down her shoulder, exposing the unblemished white flesh and a delicate collarbone. She had been careful until she pinned it into place, at which point she felt secure. She wasn't the kind of woman who gave much thought to her allure. Maybe she didn't even really know there *was* allure.

She came back carrying a fresh bucket of water, and knelt again. Zane told himself to close his eyes and concentrate on something else. But he didn't. His gaze fell, once again, on the gaping neckline of the T-shirt he'd brought her. Utterly unaware, she focused on the task at hand, kneeling beside the bed with the bucket beside her on the floor.

Her body turned and slid into a little sideways dip to rinse the washcloth. Just a small shift, but it was enough to make the shirt gape, and from his position above her, he saw the smooth white swell of a breast in a velvet bra. Incredibly perfect skin against the allure of that soft fabric.

Again. And again. And again. A glimpse of breast, then her hands sliding up his thigh, around and down, and up and around. Another glimpse and her hands slid down, rinsing flesh that had not been touched in endless months.

Finally, he did close his eyes, and his hand fisted, but there was no escape from the slow, erotic movement of her hand on his thigh. With a quick move, he reached out and caught her delicate wrist in his hand. "Stop," he growled through gritted teeth. "I'll take it from here," he said, and knew she heard the rasp in his words.

"Oh!"

Zane opened his eyes to see the blush creep from her chest to her cheeks as she realized—everything. She made a move to stand up, but somehow, he couldn't make himself release her. She stood up, anyway, as if her hand was not a part of her. She halted, half standing, when she realized he didn't mean to let her go.

The shirt gaped widely. Zane felt something selfish push through him and knew he'd set her up for this, for the slight bend that revealed everything. He stared hard at her face for a long moment, daring himself to let her go. He felt the tension in her arm, the clutch of her fingers against his thigh. Her eyes were lowered, and her cheeks flamed.

And still he didn't release her. He let his eyes move downward, toward the promise of the creamy swells of breast edging his peripheral vision. "Look at me," he said.

She tried to be defiant. Her chin tilted and her mouth was hard, but he saw more. Her pupils were so dilated she looked drugged, and there was the faint flare of her nostrils, anger and desire mingled into one betraying gesture. Her gaze flickered down to his mouth. He told himself he would only look as far as her mouth, and let himself remember that kiss, but once he lowered his gaze, he was lost.

The gaping shirt revealed a lot more from this position. The entire, erotic expanse of that velvet bra, embracing the breasts that nearly spilled free. "That's the sexiest damned thing I've ever seen," he said, and with his free hand, unfastened the safety pin.

"I don't recall inviting you to a private viewing."

"Didn't you?" He took her hand and pulled her back down, kneeling as she had been a moment before, with her hands sliding all over his thigh. Her chin lifted even higher, and he saw her breath was coming in short, hot bursts. Anger.

And desire.

Her reaction fueled his blind, selfish need, and deliberately he trailed his fingers down her neck and lightly traced the shelf of collarbone. She didn't move, but against his thumb, he felt the convulsive action of a swallow. Slowly, giving her time to stop him, he slid his fingers beneath the edge of her shirt, and beneath the velvety softness of the bra straps on each side.

Her eyes fluttered closed as he pushed the shirt down her arms, taking the delectable bra with it. His breath left him as he watched her flesh being exposed an inch at a time. The narrow shoulders, the graceful collarbone and slim upper arms. The rise of breasts cupped in velvet, not large, but creamy and white and supple. He paused in anticipation, then spread his fingers over the exposed skin. A shudder rippled through her, and the action was so arousing, Zane could not resist—he curled his fingers around the edge of fabric still covering her and pulled it away, trapping her arms at her sides in a tangle of garments.

Aware of hurried breath and her fingers unfurling on his bare thigh, he touched her, looked at her. Beautiful. Excruciatingly arousing, the way she allowed him to

simply look at the proud thrust of naked breasts, then
touch with the very tips of his fingers, and then his
whole hand, gauging the glorious soft weight in his
palms.

"Your skin is softer than feathers," he whispered,
and let her wrist go, so he could fill both hands with
the glory of that soft, supple flesh.

And she didn't stop him. He cupped her loosely,
rubbing the aroused tips against the heart lines of his
palms. His fingers looked rough and dark against the
tenderness of her skin, and something about the con-
trast—male to female, made him faintly dizzy. He bent
his head, feeling his hair fall around his face, and
kissed one pearled tip, kissed it, then touched it with
his tongue, and finally, slowly and with great gusto,
opened his mouth and sucked the sensitive flesh into
his mouth.

A quiver and a sigh passed through her. She made
a move, discovered she was trapped, and struggled to
take the sleeves from her arms. At last she was successful, and she lifted her arms to his hair. He raised
his head, ready to meet her in a kiss, but she was not
thinking of him. In a gesture as erotic as anything he'd
ever seen, she pulled his hair across her face and pulled
it over her neck, stroking her skin with the strands.

He uttered a low curse and hauled her upward, to
straddle his lap. "You're incredible, Claire," he whispered, and pulled her hard into him, her legs around
his waist, her bare torso enfolded against his arms and
chest. In a rhythm as old as time, she moved her hips,
and he groaned at the pleasure of it.

He kissed her throat, kissed the swell of her pretty
breasts, stroked her long back and—

Suddenly, there was a sound outside, a slammed

door and a cry. Zane froze, unwillingly wrenched into the present and the utter insanity of what they were doing.

"It's nothing," she said, her hands on his buttons. "Just the family next door."

He put his hands on hers. "Stop, Claire." An inferno burned under his skin and he hated himself for it, hated that he had been unable to keep his hands away, that he didn't have enough self-control to avoid seducing an innocent who would be wounded by it. "This is crazy."

She blinked, her blue eyes misty with desire, and raised her head. "What?"

A swell of fierce need pushed through him, and fighting it, he grabbed her wrists, pulling them away from his shirt, a gesture that only arched her back, putting her breasts all too close to his mouth. He gritted his teeth. "Stop."

Her face flamed scarlet instantly, and with the surprising, tensile strength she had displayed once before, she wrenched free, scrambling off him, tugging at her clothes. And then, so quickly, he had no chance to react or stop her, she bent over, grabbed the ice bucket filled with soap and hot water—

And dumped it over his head. "Go to hell, Zane Hunter," she said, then pulled her clothes into place and bolted.

Chapter 6

Claire yanked open the door blindly, her breath stuck in her lungs, her face on fire, her clothes not quite straight. Faced with the pouring rain, she halted. There was no place for her to go. For one stunned, burning moment, she simply stared at it.

And then, behind her, Zane began to laugh.

She slammed the door and turned back, crossing her arms. "I'm glad you find it so amusing," she said.

He was wet. Very wet. The water soaked his hair and his shirt, and a good portion of the bed behind him. He wiped water out of his eyes and grinned at her. "I deserved that."

"You certainly did."

He bowed his head for a moment. "I'm sorry, all right?"

Claire moved her shoulders, feeling dangerously emotional, and still aroused, and humiliated. "Don't play with me."

"It's not play, Claire." He lifted his chin, and the pine green gaze pinned her where she stood, the expression sober and sincere. "I really can't seem to stop imagining how much I'd like to make love with you."

"Have sex with, you mean," she said, and crossed her arms more tightly, her face growing hotter as she remembered the way she'd just sat there and let him humiliate her because she'd been dying for him to touch her. For a minute there, she'd really thought she could practically have climaxed with nothing more than the feel of his hands on her breasts. She squeezed her eyes tight and turned away. What was happening to her?

"Maybe," he said. "Maybe it would be better than that." He swallowed. "But whatever we call it, it's the wrong move. We're all hepped up from the situation and not thinking with rational parts of our minds, and falling into bed just because we happen to be handy is a very bad idea. Especially under those circumstances."

Claire blinked, uncertain whether she could trust this sudden rationality. And damn him, anyway. "I can't figure you out," she said suddenly. "One minute you're Mr. Nice Guy, the next you're a jerk."

"I know. I'm sorry." He sighed. "Give me a hand, will you?"

"So you can humiliate me again?" She rolled her eyes. "Get up yourself."

A half smile quirked over that beautiful mouth, but he put his hand down and struggled to his feet, gingerly, as if he wasn't sure how it would feel. Slowly, he shifted his weight to the newly revealed leg—and it promptly buckled.

Claire flew across the small space to help him, and

he grabbed her shoulders. "It's a little weaker than I expected," he said, and looked up, an oddly vulnerable expression on his face. Their eyes met, and a frisson of awareness and understanding and something deeper passed between them.

And just like that, she found her anger dissipating. He sighed and, gripping her shoulder for balance, pressed his forehead to hers. "Every time I look at you," he said, "I want to kiss you."

An almost dizzying sense of connection pulsed through her, from that small joining between their foreheads. "Me, too," Claire whispered in confession.

"And the terrible truth is, I'm a wandering man with nothing more than the clothes on my back, and there you are with your safe and settled world, and it's the wrong thing for both of us."

A twist of something—regret?—pushed through her, and in an old defensive move she'd nearly forgotten, she made a joke. "Is that a turtle story?"

But instead of laughing, he went utterly still, and she felt restraint in his wrists and the tension of his fingers. "One kiss, Claire, and then we'll promise there will be no more." He raised his head. "Okay?"

"Okay," she whispered.

Neither of them closed their eyes, so there was a dual shock of joining when their lips met, a wave of heat and need slamming her from his lips and the blur of his green eyes. He made a sound of pain as their lips opened, and he gripped her neck more tightly, tilting his head. Claire flowed into him, putting her body against his gently, feeling again the surprise of his size, and the strength in his torso and thighs even as her lips opened in welcome to his gentle, erotic tongue. In seconds, they were both breathing hard, and Claire found the presence of mind to pull away. Gently but firmly. "No more," she managed to say.

He nodded solemnly but gripped her head. "I really am sorry," he said. "I won't cross that line again."

Claire pulled away. "Thank you."

Dinner was quiet. They ate later than most of the other occupants of the motel, and the weather was grim enough that there were no travelers stopping in on their way to someplace else. Claire ate a hot beef sandwich and Zane had a hamburger, and neither of them had much to say. Claire felt vaguely awkward and even more than a little depressed. How had she ended up here, with this man, so far from home? She didn't want to be on the road, running from some nameless gunman. She wanted to be home, puttering in her kitchen, listening to her own music, sleeping in her own bed.

Only when they ordered coffee to warm them from the chill coming from the windows, did Claire raise the question that had been nagging her for hours. "Do you have any kind of plan? Or are we just going to run across Washington State for the rest of our natural lives?"

He glanced over his shoulder. The only other customers sat in a booth across the room, and although it would have taken a shout to get their attention, Zane hunched forward over his coffee and spoke in a low voice. "I have a plan. We'll lay low for another day or two, then get in touch with...uh...some people I work with and get you to a safe house in Seattle."

"How long will it be before I can go home?"

"Until I'm sure that you'll be safe."

It wasn't the answer she wanted. "If I don't get back to the inn, I'll be ruined in no time," she said. A wave of almost physical yearning washed over her as she thought of her pleasant, quiet dining room. "You have no idea how long I've worked to get it going."

"You won't be ruined," he said. "There are resources set aside for instances like this."

"Will you stop with the cloak-and-dagger stuff?"

A twinkle glinted in his eye. "But it is cloak-and-dagger."

"I thought you guys went out of business with the Cold War."

"Hell, no. Always need a good cloak-and-dagger man for something." He lifted his finger toward the waitress for the check and reached into his pocket for money. He scowled. "Damn. I have to run back to the room for cash. I left it in my *wet* jeans."

Claire opened her purse. "Running is probably a little faster than you can manage at the moment." She put the credit card on the table. "I'll pay."

He tsked with exaggeration and put the credit card back in her hand. "No way, honey. First rule of cloak-and-dagger maneuvers is that you can't leave a paper trail." He shifted, ready to slide out of the booth.

"A paper trail?"

"Technically, it's an electronic trail." He tapped the credit card with one finger. "The whole world is networked by these numbers nowadays. You use a credit card, an ATM machine, anything like that, and it is instantly recorded. Which means any fairly competent hacker can get the information—which would lead right to this spot."

Horrified, Claire said, "Zane, I used this card when we got here."

"What?"

"I used the card. For gas and all that at the convenience store."

He looked puzzled. "Convenience store?"

"You were asleep. I went there just before we came to this motel."

"This morning? In town?"

Claire could only nod.

He rubbed his face and looked out the window to the torrential rain. "Damn," he said softly.

"Is that bad?"

He took a breath. "It's not your fault. You didn't know. But yeah, it's bad. Do you have enough cash on you to pay that bill?"

"Maybe." She dug through various pockets and managed to cover the bill plus tip by scrounging quarters and dimes and nickels from various hidden seams.

"You mean you don't have a little shoe-shaped coin purse, Miss Manners?"

"Not a shoe," she said, and pulled out a tiny beaded bag with a zipper. Empty. "I just forget to use it."

He leaned heavily on her shoulder as they carried the check and cash to the register. The waitress hurried over. "Was everything all right?"

"Very good," Zane said. "Keep the change."

She smiled broadly at him, and Claire didn't miss the slight flirtatious tilt of her head. "Can you tell us what the forecast is?" she asked, finding she was a little annoyed.

"Rain, rain and more rain," she said, straightening. "Clear through Christmas Eve. It's supposed to stop by then."

"Any roads out?" Zane asked.

"Not that I've heard of." She waved toward the window. "Don't let this alarm you, folks. We always flood a little right here. Things are likely fine once you get on the main roads.''

"Great. Thanks." He leaned heavily on Claire. "Maybe we ought to get a few supplies to tide us over, just in case."

"In case of what?"

"Just…in case."

"What are we going to use for money?" she asked.

A shrug. "Our whereabouts are known right now, so we'll just use the card. Won't hurt anything now." He paused. "Unless you mind. You will be reimbursed."

"I don't mind."

He pointed out bottles of water, chocolate bars, peanut butter, crackers—things Claire associated with hiking. It puzzled her until she realized what they really meant—survival supplies. A burst of fear unsettled her stomach. Her hand trembled when she handed the man her credit card.

Zane didn't seem to notice.

Back in the room, he said, "Get your things together. We've got to get out of here." He tossed his few things in a pile, then stood in the middle of the room, eyeing the phone. "I'll be back in a minute," he said. "I have to make a phone call."

The pay phone was located under a deep porch, but Zane had to hunch around it, anyway, using his body to block the blowing rain. In seconds, he was shivering and wet, his bad leg aching all the way through to the marrow.

And standing there, soaking wet and miserable and hurting, he stared bleakly at the gray metal numeric keypad. He felt isolated and inexpressibly weary—

weary of slipping from one place to another, his entire life an exercise in anonymity and lies. He couldn't remember, standing there in the rain, why he'd believed in this life once. Why he'd ever believed he'd done any good, or when he'd stopped being one of the good guys and become a hunter with a gun in his hand and nothing to lose.

But the game had gone on so long now, he had no choice but to see it through. He picked up the receiver and punched in a series of codes, waiting for the clicks and electronic signals that prompted him for further codes. After a long, static-filled pause, a line rang. And to his relief, a man with a musical, accented voice answered. "Hello."

"Damn, it's good to hear your voice," Zane said.

"Ho! Where in blazes are you? The whole Organization is in an uproar over your disappearance."

"If I told you, you wouldn't know any more than you do now—some little town in Washington State." He paused, knowing Max would do whatever was necessary to help him, and wondered how far to go. "Look, man, I'm in trouble."

"I'm listening."

"I've got a civilian with me, a woman, and the Ghost has found me. We're about to get out of Dodge, but I'll need some backup in a few days. Can I count on you?"

"Of course."

"It's got to be just us, man. I've been ordered off this case, but I'll be damned if I'll let anyone else take her down."

"Her?"

"The Ghost is a woman. See what you can call up

out of HQ files on French women in the intelligence community. Somebody had to train her, somewhere.''

"French? Are you certain?"

"Yeah." A gust of wind soaked his back once again, and Zane clenched his teeth against the onslaught. "I gotta get out of here. I'll call you back tomorrow or the next day to get that background and let you know when and where I need you."

"Good, good." A pause. "Be careful."

"Always, man. Always." He hung up and turned toward the wind to go back to Claire. Icy rain pricked his forehead and cheekbones and chin, and he wished for a heavier coat. Across the parking lot, he saw Claire come out of the room, Coach trailing happily behind her. She staggered a moment in a gust of wind, then pushed forward and dropped her load into the back seat, then pushed it back. Coach eagerly jumped in, his tongue lolling.

At least she had a good down parka, he thought. And there were blankets in the truck if they needed them.

Using the umbrella as a cane, he made his way over, glanced into the motel room to satisfy himself that it was empty, then joined her in the truck. Her face was white, and he had not missed the trembling of her hands in the shop. A part of him longed to reach out and cover those small hands with his own. The more rational side, intent on her survival, kept him still.

"Zane," she said. "I'm sorry."

He shook his head. "It's not your fault. You couldn't know."

She started the car. "Where to?"

"Hell, I don't know. Drive somewhere. The important thing is not the location, just that we clear out of here."

"Do you want me to head toward Seattle or toward the coast? To Oregon, or toward Canada?" An edge of hysteria made her voice crack, and Zane watched her work her fingers around the steering wheel so tightly that the knuckles were bloodless. "I don't know what to do."

"You're right." He blew out a sigh. "Not Seattle. Not yet. I have to get my leg in working order first. Go…west. To the coast, I guess."

Again he was impressed with her driving. Rain came down in sheets, and even the highest setting on the windshield wipers couldn't entirely keep up. With the wind and the rain, the noise was intense, and to make it all truly nightmarish, the roads were beginning to flood. Claire managed it all without a complaint, though he could tell her shoulders were aching with the effort. "I hope we drive out of this soon," she said finally. "But I guess if it's this bad, it will be just as bad for the bad guy, huh?"

"Right." He touched her shoulder, unable to resist, and felt the ungiving steel corded from neck to arm. He told himself she'd earned a shoulder rub when they got somewhere safe.

For a while, it did seem to get better. They reached higher ground and drove through the thick darkness of a forest. The rain still fell relentlessly, but the roaring subsided as trees took the brunt of the wind. Claire pushed a cassette into the tape player, and classical music filled the cab.

"I like this," Zane said. "Who is it?"

"Boccherini," she said. "A minuet."

"Is that a dance or something?"

Through the darkness, he saw her smile. "Yes. From

the eighteenth century, very stylized. But I like the happiness in the music.''

In a self-mocking tone, he said, ''Where I come from, if it ain't got drums, it ain't for dancing.''

She chuckled. ''And where I come from—'' her voice turned to hayseed country ''—if you ain't country, you ain't nothing.''

''Aha. Another clue. You're a Southern country girl.''

A pause. A sigh. ''Arkansas.''

''Hmmm. And why bother to hide that?''

''I don't know. It's just gotten to be a habit.'' She scaled a steep right turn smoothly, then added, ''I was ashamed of where I came from, probably. I was afraid nobody would take me seriously if they knew.''

''Hell, honey, the president of the United States is a native of Arkansas.''

''I know. But he's Southern genteel, which is a whole 'nother category.''

''Yeah?''

''Yes, sir. I seriously doubt there's any spot quite as class-conscious as the American South. Trust me, everybody knows which part of town you're born to, and it takes an act of God to change it.'' She shook her head, and he wondered if he knew how her chin lifted, as if in defiance, when she said ''Or you can move away.'' As if it had been a victory to accomplish it.

''And what category do you hail from?''

''Oh, I guess I'd have to say poor white trash.''

The words, so very harsh, hung in the air for a long moment. Zane didn't want to interrupt anything she might add, and stayed silent. But unlike most people, she added nothing else. Her lips were clamped tight, her gaze hard on the road ahead. He thought, unaccountably, of her curling up so comfortably with her dog in the back seat, and of the way she had managed the terror of that night with such calm.

Finally he said, "That's a pretty harsh summation."

"Yep." A half beat. "It's also true."

"Why do you say that?"

"Oh, I don't know, Zane," she drawled, and he heard edges of bitterness, maybe even anger. "What comes up for you when I say that?"

"Nothing. A stereotype."

"Yeah? And what's the stereotype?" She spared a sharp glance at him. "What do you think of?"

He shifted, uncomfortable, but recognized that he'd started this conversation and it was only fair to follow it through. He let go of a breath and inclined his head. "Trailer parks, I guess. A rusty car or two up on blocks in the yard, young girls with babies and cigarettes in their hands."

"Bingo," she said.

"That's where you grew up, in a trailer park?"

"Sure did. Not even a double-wide." The sharp ironic note in her voice made him hurt a little.

"Big parts of the reservations look like that, too, you know." He paused, remembering. "A trailer is affordable housing in a lot of places. There's no shame in that. No shame in coming from anywhere."

"Sure, Zane. Whatever you say."

"That sounds pretty bitter for a woman who managed to make a pretty nice life for herself." He inclined his head. "There's nothing to be ashamed of in poverty."

"No." She said it quietly, but there was still an edge of hardness to the word. "Not in the poverty. But sometimes there's a lot to be ashamed of in what that poverty does to a person. And it does matter, Zane, where you come from. It takes a lot of work to overcome that kind of background.''

"Most people don't," he said quietly, thinking of her cozy inn—and with a piercing realization—her Christmas tree. "You have a lot to be proud of."

"I've worked hard, that's all."

"Takes more than that, Claire, and you know it. It takes grit. You have that in spades."

"Do I?"

He chuckled. "You haven't been hysterical one time in all of this." He shifted, putting his shoulder against the door so he could look at her. "You've been pissed off."

She nodded. "Yes."

"And you've been frightened."

"Oh, yeah."

"And you've been determined to get through it. But no panic. You'd probably be a hell of an agent."

"Pass." She glanced at him. "But while we're on the subject of reality, why don't you give me a little clue about what's really going on with you? What's the real story? Who are you working for, and who is on your trail?"

He took a breath, considering.

"Fair is fair, Zane Hunter," she said. "I nearly always lie about my background, and I told you the truth."

Intrigued, he grinned. "Yeah? What kind of lie?"

She lifted her shoulders, her eyes on the road. "All kinds of them, really. I guess my favorite has to be the one where my daddy was a decorated Vietnam veteran who died from Agent Orange diseases and my mama was old money and got disinherited when she fell in love with that soldier in his uniform.''

He laughed softly. ''I like it.''

She looked at him. ''Now you.''

''All right.'' He could at least give her the gist of it—she was in so deep it didn't really matter. Sooner or later, she'd know most of it. ''I can't tell you who I work for—''

''Not fair!''

He held up a hand. ''Let me finish, will you?''

''Oh. Okay.''

''I can't tell you who I work for because it's a top-secret, private organization that works with a lot of different intelligence agencies all over the world.''

''Isn't private intelligence sort of an oxymoron?''

''Not really. It was created with goals of peace and prevention in mind by...'' He halted, knowing she'd like the story of Joshua Purcell, an eccentric billionaire who'd come by his idealism honestly in the turbulent sixties and set out to make a fortune so he could devote himself to peace.

But there were guidelines. ''Let's just leave it at that, and I'll tell you my part.''

''All right.''

''My father was a cop, but that didn't really pay a lot, so on the weekends during the fall and winter, he used to take hunting parties out into the mountains and help them track game. I always went with him—he even bought me a hound that had the best nose in twelve counties. After my dad died and my mom got religion—'' he gave her a half smile ''—it was me and Zeke, up in the mountains, tracking things.''

''You had a dog named Zeke?'' She glanced at him. ''Mine was Jake.''

"No kidding. What kind of dog?"

A shrug. "Just mutt, probably mostly terrier, with a little shepherd. I picked Coach because his colors are the same. He was my best friend." She gave him a sad little smile. "Sometimes my only friend."

"Me, too," he said quietly. "I still miss that dog sometimes."

"I did," she confessed, "until I got Coach. That's what you need—another dog."

"No room in my life right now for a pup." But the idea had a strange appeal. A dog was a good companion. No matter what, it was there, waiting, solidly in your corner.

"Which leads back to the original question, Mr. Slippery Conversationalist. Dogs don't have anything to do with what's going on now."

"That's where you're wrong. Because, it was thanks to Zeke that I got my reputation. We were good—not only with tracking deer and antelope, but other things, too. Sometimes a bear that was coming into town too often. A bobcat that mauled some local dogs. We even found a body one time that had been lost for a month."

"Yuck."

"Yeah." He didn't add that he'd been called upon more and more often as nearby Denver produced its share of missing persons. It wasn't the only body he'd ever found. "I liked finding the live ones a lot better. When I was about nineteen or twenty, a senator was stumping in Denver, and his wife and kid went on a picnic. The kid got lost, and they brought me in to find him."

"If this has a sad ending, I'm not in the mood to hear it."

"No. It took three days, but I found him. He was

miserable. He was scared speechless, and he didn't let me go for two hours after I got him back to town, but he was alive. It got a lot of press.''

Until then, Zane had been nobody from nowhere. He was a mixed-blood Blackfoot in a community made up mainly of Sioux who had drifted down from the reservations. In his mother's world, he was exotic. He'd been alienated and bristling with a bad attitude, headed nowhere fast.

''A man came to see me. Said he'd give me training and plenty of money if I'd come to work for him, tracking people for him.'' He shrugged. ''I said yes. And that's what I've been doing ever since.''

''And this person who's after you, it's somebody you were tracking?''

''Yes.'' He paused to give weight to his next words. ''She's an assassin, and very good. She will kill me— and you with me—if she can, because if she doesn't, I'll kill her first.''

Claire was silent for a long moment. ''Is she connected to your injury?''

''She set the bomb,'' he said flatly. ''Killed two of my friends instead of me.''

''I'm sorry.''

As if to make a mockery of the conversation of bombs and death, the music, light and free, almost exuberant, distracted Zane. ''What music is this now?''

''Bruch.''

''It sounds like it's from a movie or something,'' he commented, leaning back, the weight of his choices and his life pressing down against his chest. ''Like any minute, some babe in a sequined dress and rhinestones flashing in her eyes will come out dancing and steal away the hero's heart.''

Her laughter—surprised and somehow full-throated—burst from her, and Zane found himself looking toward her. "It does sound like that," she said. "They must have used it in some of those old forties movies."

She drove around a curve and onto a bridge. The tires made a hollow thunking sound against the wood, and she slowed down. Zane looked idly out his window to the stream, then sat up straight.

"Go!" he cried "Get off the bridge!"

"What? I am—"

The sound reached them, at last. They might have heard it sooner if they had not been cocooned in the vehicle, with classical music playing and the patter of rain on the roof. It was a rushing roar, unmistakable. Water, rushing, carrying in its mouth a swell of debris carted off the banks and perhaps even some of the towns in the area. Zane stared with horror at the wall of water headed toward them, carrying in the froth a monstrous tree branch. He thought of the rain-gorged rivers of his childhood, and the havoc they could wreak. "Flash flood," he said. "Drive, damn it!"

Chapter 7

Claire saw the water rushing toward the little bridge and stomped her foot down hard on the gas, hard enough to send the rear fishtailing over the wet wooden bridge. She steered into the swerve and righted it, but didn't dare let up on the speed.

She could hear the roar of the approaching wall, and a zinging electricity sparked up her spine as she attempted to outrun it, trying not to think of the water knocking them off the bridge, into the—

No. She would rather be shot than drown.

The front tires grabbed the road on the other side of the bridge, and at the same instant, an explosion of sound roared out behind them. Claire cried out with the effort of holding on to the wheel, her foot hard on the accelerator as water sucked the tail of the truck. For one long, agonizing moment, she fought the sucking water for control, her hands tight on the wheel, her foot so hard on the gas she thought her knee would break. "Come on, baby! Come on!"

With a grinding sound, the truck won the tug-of-war, and they pulled free of the overflowing creek. The sudden thrust carried them fifty feet before Claire regained control and slowed, then stopped, her heart pounding with sickening thuds, her hands trembling violently. She put her head on the steering wheel and let go of a breath.

"Whoo!" Zane cried out, and slapped her shoulder with almost jarring force. "That was something, kiddo!"

She raised her head and looked behind her. There was nothing much to see but the rushing water. The bridge was gone.

"You are one incredible woman."

Against her will, she grinned. His delight in beating the odds was irresistible. "Thanks."

He reached forward, grabbed her face and kissed her hard. "That was great, Claire." He pulled back so fast she barely had time to react.

"Well, if you don't mind, I think I'm going to stop at the first motel we see. That scared ten years off my life."

But in actuality, it was three towns farther west before Zane let her stop. The first town was too small, not much more than a fish-and-tackle store, a gas station and a decidedly seedy motel that likely catered to hunting buddies. A bar next door flashed a red neon sign into the rainy night.

The second, a parochially neat town with swept sidewalks and pristine curtains hanging at every window, was too "mid-America," Zane pronounced. They'd stand out like sore thumbs. Claire drove on.

At last, nearly fifty miles beyond the washed-out bridge, Claire said, "Any minute now, we'll be driving into the Pacific. I want to stop here."

He peered out the windows, and she realized she could read the faintest agitation in his extraordinary stillness. She slowed down, letting him take measure of the place. It was larger than the other two towns they'd driven through, and catered to the ocean views it boasted. The theme seemed to be Ultimate Northwest; all the buildings were constructed of unpainted, rugged-looking wood. They passed a good-size supermarket, three churches, several blocks of businesses—including some decent-looking motels.

Finally, Claire said, "I'm not driving another mile. Decide which one you want, as long as it says it has cable television, and let's go there. I desperately want a hot shower and a good movie."

The hard line of his jaw loosened minutely, and he let go of a heavy breath. "Good idea. Pull into the liquor store first, and we'll find a room. Are you hungry?"

"Not at all." She pulled into the liquor store parking lot, and Zane got out. She turned off the lights and the windshield wipers, but left the truck running for the heat. The tape had finished just as they drove into town, and now the world was almost preternaturally silent.

She stared at multicolored Christmas bulbs around the liquor store window, at the fake snow lettering that advertised six packs of premium beer for $4.99, and for one bleak moment, she was transported again to childhood. To a little girl sitting in the back seat of a car while her mother blew all her tips on whatever liquor her current boyfriend preferred.

In the darkness and quiet, the past two days caught

up with her, and Claire fought a wave of blackest despair. It worked its way up from her belly, cold and devouring, sucking at the air in her lungs and snaking up her throat to choke her.

She flung open the car door and stumbled into the rain, letting the cold splash her face, soak her hair, bring her back to the present. To now.

It worked. She tipped her face up to the sky and gritted her teeth and her fists and forced the specter of the past away. She would never be at the mercy of someone else's whims as long as she lived.

The helplessness of the current situation was dredging up old memories. At the very heart of the past two day's events was that one, unavoidable fact: she was helpless, more or less, dependent upon the kindness of a stranger. Just the sort of melodrama her mother had loved, a melodrama with the beautiful, downtrodden woman at its heart. Too bad those plays had never ended happily, Claire thought now.

But she was not her mother. She had learned to make her own luck, and even now, she wouldn't depend on this stranger for anything except the barest direction.

He came out of the store and a bell rung. Seeing Claire, he stopped, leaning on his cane for support, a brown paper bag under the other arm. "Are you all right?" he asked.

Claire turned her head, and all the repressed anger of the past two days bubbled up in a rush. "No, damn it, I'm really not all right! How could I be? I think this really sucks, if you want to know the truth. I like my house. I *love* my house. I've worked my ass off for a little security, and it infuriates me that I'm out here in the middle of nowhere eating disgusting food, fighting rivers and dodging bullets instead of sitting in my warm, comfortable living room in front of a fire.''

''Such language!'' He winked at her. ''That's my girl.''

''And I'm not a girl, either, Mr. Hunter.''

He made his way to the passenger door. ''You're right,'' he said. ''I apologize.'' Rain trickled down his face, and colored lights from the windows shone on the carved planes—a line of blue down the straight nose, an arc of red on his cheekbone. ''I'd be more than happy to argue this out, but can we do it somewhere a little warmer?''

Knowing she was behaving foolishly, Claire nonetheless rolled her eyes and climbed into the truck. The sudden warmth hit her hands like needles, and she realized she was going to soak the cloth seats.

Zane climbed in from the other side and made a shivering noise. ''It's getting really cold!''

Claire nodded. Her body tingled, head to toe, a sign that she was alive. That she'd beat back the demon of despair one more time. ''Let's get somewhere where we can get showers and warm up. Maybe we can order a pizza or something.''

''I thought you weren't hungry?''

''A woman is entitled to change her mind, Mr. Secret Agent Man.''

''Good enough.''

At the Ocean Overlook Motel, Claire pulled in beneath an awning. Impossible to tell in the dark and the rain if the name was correct, but it looked well kept, and the sign boasted free cable and HBO in every room. ''I don't suppose we could have separate rooms?'' Claire asked as Zane prepared to get out.

"I can ask for connecting, if you like. No offense, but you strand me out here, and I'm dead. And I don't like the idea of letting you out of my sight just yet. Not until I'm certain you're safe."

"I'm not in any hurry to get myself killed, Zane," she said with some impatience. "I just want some privacy."

His eyes rested soberly on her face for a moment. "I'll see what I can do."

When he climbed back into the truck, he was whistling. "Number twenty, over there in the corner," he said.

"They didn't have two rooms?"

"Better than that." He gestured as the headlights swept over the building. "Voilà!" he said, in what sounded to Claire like a very good accent.

It was a small cabin, complete with a porch. Following Zane inside, she saw with pleasure that there was a small living room-kitchen area, and a bedroom to one side. A small Christmas tree, decorated with various kinds of angel ornaments, perfumed the air from one corner. Claire glanced away.

"The couch turns into a bed," he explained. "You can have the bedroom and I'll sleep out here. And look—" he moved to the counter and gestured with a game-show-host grin "—a coffeemaker."

Sudden gratitude made her feel overwhelmed. "Thank you, Zane. I'm sorry I was ugly out there. I just—"

He shook his head. "Nothing to apologize for." He pointed toward the door to the bathroom. "You can shower first. I'll bring our stuff in."

"Don't be ridiculous. You're handicapped. You take the shower and I'll bring stuff in."

"No." His voice was unexpectedly firm. Almost harsh. She glanced at him in surprise. "Let me have a little dignity, huh?"

She shrugged. "Fine. Are you going to call for a pizza, too?"

"Sure." He grinned. "I'll even find out what's on the movie channel."

Claire again felt that sense of intense gratitude pushing at her walls. "Thanks," she said, and hurried to the bathroom, feeling uneasily fragile. The last thing in the world that she wanted was to let her protective walls crack any further than they already had, leaving her vulnerable and exposed to the kindness of a stranger who might be dead next week.

By the time the pizza—a huge combination—was delivered, Claire felt a lot more like herself. Warm, dry and relieved to be somewhere safe, she tackled the pizza with a voracious appetite, then made a pot of coffee with two of the cellophane packages tucked into a basket on the counter. "Hey," she called out, examining the other offerings in the basket. "This is terrific. Did you see the jams and jellies, and the cookies?"

"Biscuits," Zane said from the couch. His leg was propped on a low table, and she saw him rubbing the knee when he thought she didn't notice. "They're English shortbreads, so technically, they're biscuits."

Claire shook her head in mock despair. "No, sugar," she said in an exaggerated drawl, "biscuits are those fluffy, tender things I serve my guests for Sunday morning breakfast. This here's a cookie." She opened the package and took out a chocolate-dipped shortbread. Examining it in anticipation, she said, "That's something you'll miss out on, Mr. Hunter, my Sunday breakfast spread.''

"If it is anywhere close to as good as that soup, I'm very sorry I will."

"Oh, that soup is nothing. I serve a real Southern-style breakfast on Sunday mornings. Sausage, smoked bacon and sliced ham, with country potatoes, grits, scrambled eggs, homemade biscuits and even gravy."

He made a noise of sorrowful pain. "Remind me to come back when I can stay over on Sunday."

"I'll do that," she answered, knowing a woman like her would never call a man like Zane Hunter. Shrugging off the heaviness of the thought, she leaned on the counter as the coffeemaker started its noisy brewing process. She bit into the cookie. Tender, buttery crumbs and dark chocolate fell into her mouth. "Oooh, that's good. You want one?"

"Maybe in a little while." His mouth showed a thin white line all the way around, as it had when he first arrived at her inn.

"You need something for that ache, Mr. Hunter? I have ibuprofen in my handbag."

"Please," he said.

"You don't look too good," she said, carrying the pills to him. "Maybe you ought to just get some rest."

"Nah. I'll be all right. A little brandy, some pain-killers, and I'll be set."

"Brandy or ibuprofen," she said, taking the pills back. "Not both."

"Do you have any aspirin in that magic bag?" He asked. "Aspirin and brandy should be all right."

"It'll tear up your stomach but shouldn't kill you." And although it was not her inn, and she was not re-quired, she poured coffee for both of them into substantial, heavy mugs she found in the cupboard, arranged some cookies on a plate, then put all of it on a tray and carried it to the living area.

"You don't have to wait on me, Claire. It's probably better if you don't, so I can get this leg back to normal as quickly as possible."

She settled the tray on the low coffee table. "Tomorrow, I'll hike you up and down cliffs if you want. Tonight—" she poured a heavy measure of brandy into a highball glass and handed it to him "—you need to give yourself a break."

A stillness entered his green eyes as he accepted the offering. Claire glimpsed a measuring, probing expression before she turned away and busied herself with her own coffee. She leaned back gingerly in her corner, propping her stocking feet on the table beside the tray, and tried to appear relaxed.

"Aren't you going to have a little with me?" he asked. "It's very good brandy."

"Ah, no thanks." The look of it in his glass was deeply tempting, and she knew her aching shoulders would welcome the relaxation, but she feared letting down her guard. He looked sexy and clean and eminently devourable, sitting there on the couch, his hair tumbling around his shoulders. She needed her inhibitions firmly in place. "I'll just get my sugar fix from chocolate."

"Do you have issues over alcohol?"

"Issues?" She grinned. "That's awfully politically correct, Mr. Secret Agent Man."

He inclined his head, his eyes serious. "You were very upset at the liquor store, then declined the brandy, and I realized I haven't seen you drink. It's a fair question."

Claire sipped her coffee and sidestepped the truth. "I like a glass of wine or brandy now and then. Just not tonight."

"Mmm." He shifted, putting his feet on the floor and his glass on the table. "Come here, then, and let me give you a shoulder rub. I could tell in the car that those muscles were tighter than steel wire."

Alarm shot through her. "A shoulder rub?" she echoed blankly.

He smiled. "No liberties, I promise." The grin widened. "Unless you specifically request it."

"Thanks, but no thanks." His hands would definitely be more intoxicating than the brandy. "I'm fine. Really."

"Claire," he said firmly. "Come sit over here now. If you don't do one or the other, you'll sleep so tight you'll have a headache in the morning."

He was right. Her neck and shoulders ached from gripping the wheel for hours in bad weather. "Oh, all right," she said, and abruptly she stood up. "But no funny business."

"Scout's honor."

She settled in front of him. "Were you ever a Boy Scout?"

"No." He chuckled.

"That's what I figured." Tucking her feet under her, she moved her hair sideways, feeling air touch her oddly vulnerable nape. An instant later, his hands fell on her shoulders. She didn't jump and was proud of herself for that.

But that was as long as she stayed aloof. His hands were large and very strong, and the minute he started kneading the knotted muscles, she let go of a heartfelt groan and leaned back into the expert massage. "Oh, yeah," she said quietly, and closed her eyes.

"I knew it would feel good," he remarked quietly, but said no more.

Claire didn't speak, either, just closed her eyes and gave herself up to his expert ministrations. Tension sprang up and was kneaded away in one spot after another. He rubbed her neck, high and low, and the rocky muscles between her shoulder blades. His thumbs pressed firm spirals over every knob of her spine. After a while, she shifted her legs out from under her to be more comfortable, and let her body go limp.

And still those long fingers worked. One shoulder, then the other. Right upper arm, then left. When she was nearly as boneless as a loose hair, he spoke in a husky voice. "Lean back a little."

She obeyed as if hypnotized. His hands moved under her hair, on her scalp, finding the spots that were sore from contained stress, and he rubbed them away. He massaged her head until she was dizzy, then firmly rubbed her forehead and temples, as well.

When he finally ceased, her head lolled over his good leg, and one arm was draped over his bad one, gently. "Better?" he asked.

"You missed your calling," she said, her voice slow as warm honey. "You've got great hands."

He reached for his brandy on the table and took a swallow. "You should see what else I can do with them."

Claire smiled, as she knew she was meant to do, and with great effort, used her jellylike limbs to move away and haul herself up on the couch beside him. "Men are such braggarts," she said.

"Some are bragging, I suppose." He lifted his eyebrows wickedly, then nudged her with the glass. "Taste it. It won't hurt you."

In this mellow mood, Claire could not resist. Lifting her head, she acquiesced, tasting a hint of pear as she swallowed. "Oh, that is *good*."

"Have some."

She shook her head, content with the warmth a sip had given. But he poured a small amount in a water glass and handed it to her. Accepting it, Claire said, "Plying me with liquor now, are you?"

"Not at all." He leaned back comfortably, one arm along the back of the couch, and propped his bad leg back on the table. "Just a nightcap for a hell of a day."

"Amen to that," Claire said, and lifted the glass in a toast before she took another teeny, tiny swallow. If she drank it slowly, she wouldn't lose her head. "I thought we were done for on that bridge."

"So did I, to tell you the truth, but it might be just what the doctor ordered in one way. If we can't get out, our enemy can't get in." He picked up the remote control and flipped channels until he found a news program out of Seattle. The newscaster was a slim, dark woman with a haughty but elegant nose. She was obviously recapping the world headlines, and Zane hit the mute button.

"That's kind of what I imagined the woman on the phone to look like," Claire said sleepily. She glanced over at him and caught a grimace of pain tightening his mouth. When he realized she was looking at him, the expression disappeared, and Claire was pierced. "You don't have to pretend you're feeling randy and aroused when you're feeling like somebody's old shoe, Zane."

Thick black lashes swept down, hiding his eyes.

"You were very nearly killed in that explosion, weren't you? It's not just your leg, either, is it?"

He lifted a shoulder. "Part of the game."

Which acknowledged the truth of her guess without giving much else away. "Why would you want to live like that?"

He raised his eyes. "I can't remember anymore, Claire," he said. "Once, it was exciting. Kind of a thrill to be part of something bigger than myself, working for a better world."

His gaze flickered away, focused on something different. "And for a long time, I didn't have any connection to the darker side of things, you know. My job was to find people in order to protect them, or find somebody who would likely kill a lot of other people if he wasn't stopped."

It sounded reasonable. "But?" she prompted.

He considered his glass, lifted it, drank a little more brandy. Not a gulp, she noticed, not for fortification, but more than likely for the flavor sliding over his tongue, down his throat. He obviously didn't let a drop slide by unnoticed. It somehow aroused her oddly, that focus, and when he looked at her, the deep pine green of his eyes fueled the feeling even more.

"But it's dangerous work," he said at last. "Sooner or later, you get your hands dirty, and it gets harder and harder to know where to draw the line. What's justifiable and what's just blood lust or anger or some bullshit rationalization."

"Why not leave, then?"

He made a soft, skeptical noise. "And do what? I've been in this game since I was twenty years old. It's not exactly a recommendation for some other line of work." He gave her an ironic smile. "References are hard to come by."

"So you plan to just stick with it until you get killed? Until a car bomb gets you or the assassin is luckier or quicker than you are?"

He stared at his glass a long time. Finally, he said, "That sums it up."

Claire sat up, frowning. "How can you just give in? Without even trying?"

"Lack of choices," he said with an edge to his voice.

"Nope." She shook her head emphatically. "Until they put you in a grave, you have choices. Why can't you resign and go back to school or something, find a new career?"

"Too old."

Claire tsked. "Nonsense."

"I understand what you're saying, Claire, but it's just not that easy."

"I don't think you do understand," she said sharply. "You have everything, don't you see? You have your mother and your health, or what's left of it, and common sense and a good brain. You have everything you need to get a better life. You just have to take it."

"You missed 'good looks.'"

Claire rolled her eyes and stood up. "Never mind," she said. "I can tell when I'm dealing with denial. It's your life. Throw it away if you want to." Carefully, she stepped around him. "I'm going to bed. Good night."

"Wait a minute." He punched the volume on the television.

Claire turned to see film footage of flood waters rushing through a canyon, trees falling from the muddy slopes to the roads below. The newscaster narrated the scenes—destruction wrought by the storms the past few days, first snow, then rain. A map of western Washington, with most of the coast blocked in red, came up. "Law enforcement officials are asking all travel to southwestern Washington be rerouted until at least Wednesday. Many bridges have been washed out, and many of the other roads have been blocked by landslides." She turned with a sad smile to her companion, a blond man with a Kennedy smile. "Not the best news for Christmas travelers, John."

"With a little luck," John answered, "they'll get it cleared up by Christmas Eve. In other news…"

"That's good news, isn't it?" Claire asked.

"It's doubtful the Ghost got through behind us," he replied. "At least for a day or two, we'll be safe."

She nodded. "Good night, then."

But as she moved toward the privacy of the bedroom, his hand snagged her wrist. "Don't go," he said. And then raised his beautiful eyes. "Please?"

Chapter 8

Zane waited, humbled, for her reply, watching emotions sail over the ocean blue of her eyes—distrust, desire, maybe even resignation—before he felt her stop tugging at her wrist. "Well, since you said please, I can hardly refuse," she said, her expression softening to something rueful. "I was just thinking it might be…safer if I left."

He wanted to open his hand, let it slide down until they were palm to palm. He resisted, moving only his thumb against the delicate skin of her inner wrist. "What's life without a little danger?"

"I don't know," she said, grinning. "Count me crazy, but danger is just not something I miss much on a day-to-day level."

He grinned. "Stick with me, kid."

"Is there anything on the movie channel?"

"Sit down and we'll look."

She relented.

They agreed on a romantic comedy. Zane found it ridiculously satisfying to sit on a slightly abused sofa, both of them in their stocking feet, eating cookies and watching movies with a woman who wore not a stitch of makeup and had forgotten to do anything with her hair when she got out of the shower. It curled slightly, springing free of the cloth thingy she used to pull it back.

It was cozy. It was comfortable. It made the world of international espionage seem like a joke.

As the brandy moved in his veins, he wanted to reach over and hold her hand, but that would promise more than it ought to, wouldn't it? Holding hands said a man had honorable intentions, that he was content to let the relationship develop at a natural pace.

There was no such thing as a natural pace for him anymore. And he had nothing to offer in the intentions department. That thought, together with her probing questions earlier, made him consider what he could do with himself if he left this gig. Money wasn't a problem; most of his expenses were paid, and he earned a hefty salary for his work. Over the years, he'd made excellent investments and socked away whatever he didn't use in an emergency fund.

So maybe it wasn't too late. Maybe he could find a nice ranch somewhere—

Ugh. Not a ranch. He knew way too much about the job to find any pleasure in that idea. A ranch, in this day and age, sucked the life from a man. Too much work and too many government regulations.

No, not a ranch. But something. Something out there would suit him, surely.

Worn by the long day, eased by the sense of safety he felt and the smell of Claire's skin in his nose, he drifted into a doze, then deeper into sleep. In that half world, he was holding Claire's hand, and she was whispering to him, whispering a joke that sounded pretty damned sexy.

He started awake to silence and bolted forward.

"Sh," Claire murmured, her hand on his chest. "I brought you an extra pillow."

Still more or less lost in that in-between world, he gazed at her sleepily. Light from the kitchen cast a halo of honey-colored light over her hair and caught with impudence on her mouth, which was upturned in a gentle smile. He touched the gold light on her hair, pressed his palm to her cheek. "You look like an angel, Claire."

She pushed the pillow against his chest. "That's me, the Christmas angel, bringing presents." She planted a delicate kiss against his brow. "Good night, Zane."

It seemed he could feel the tingle of that kiss following him well into the night, following him into his dreams.

Claire awakened early. Zane was still asleep, and on impulse, she left him a note and a full pot of coffee, then slipped out with Coach to a morning thick with fog rolling in from the ocean. She paused on the porch, admiring the misty wrappers draped over towering Douglas firs, breathing in the briny smell of the sea. In the early quiet, she could hear the waves breaking, that soft, muted rush that was so exhilarating.

She had intended to drive, but once out in the freshness of morning, the idea of a walk sounded far more appealing. She set out briskly, headed toward a grocery store she'd seen last night. Coach, on his leash, leapt up every few feet to lick her fingers in gratitude, his face wreathed in a tongue-lolling dog smile.

It made her chuckle. "Sorry," she said. "I guess life has not been exactly thrilling for you the past few days." She rubbed his head and promised, "We'll walk on the beach later. You'll love it."

Whether due to a good night's sleep and a normal schedule, or the marshaling of her demons, Claire felt surprisingly good this morning. In the grocery store, she hummed under her breath happily, picking out huge navel oranges and smoked bacon and eggs, and even a small bag of flour. There was salt and pepper in the motel kitchen, but she tossed in a can of baking powder just in case. She hadn't thought to look.

The aisles were piled with the special offerings of Christmas—nuts in their shells and baskets of fruit wrapped in cellophane. Bags of filled hard candy, peppermint sticks and ribbon candy were piled invitingly by the register. Christmas carols poured through the overhead speakers, chipper and cheerful.

Standing behind a mother with a toddler on her hip and a baby in the basket, Claire wondered what it would be like to have stockings to fill for a child. And what one put in them. Chocolate? Fruit? A friend of hers had always received a giant candy cane that she generously shared with Claire.

Her mother had not bothered with Santa Claus, saying she'd be damned if some old fat white-haired man was going to take credit for anything she'd worked her fanny off for. The memory, rather than making her feel depressed, this morning made Claire smile. Whatever else could be said about her mother, she'd been a character.

And as she eyed the flannel stockings hung in rows,

the candy canes in big piles and the magazines in their slick red covers offering hundreds of cookie recipes, holiday feasts and craft ideas, she experienced a moment of revelation. Why was Christmas any different from any other time of year? Why couldn't she build a set of holiday traditions for herself, to celebrate at the inn, year after year? She could hang stockings for herself and her dog for now, and keep some extras around for guests. Then, one day, if she was lucky enough to have a family of her own, she would have had practice.

Lifting her chin, she picked out the two most promising magazines and bought a handful of candy canes for the little tree at the cabin, and even a stocking to hang up beside it. Maybe, she thought with a faint smile, she'd put Zane's name on it.

Zane awakened to the scents of frying bacon and fresh coffee, and the absurdly pleasant sound of a woman singing under her breath. Lazily, he opened his eyes but didn't move. There was a hominess about the comfortable smells and the warmth of covers over a body that didn't seem to hurt anywhere.

Claire was busy in the kitchenette, adding bacon to a frying pan on the stove. She had tied a towel around her waist and had tugged her hair into a ponytail that bounced. He shifted on the pillow a little to get a better look at her, liking the energy of her movements and the obvious pleasure she took in the task. Best of all, he liked that breathy, almost tuneless humming. It was something his mother had done, something his father had sometimes teased her about unmercifully—a constant, airy sound as she went about her chores, drove a car, anything.

Finally the tune penetrated. "Joy to the World." Off key. Very badly off, but recognizable. He smiled to himself and sat up, shoving hair out of his face. Quietly, in a voice he knew was strong and deep, he joined in the chorus, "And heav'n and nature sing…"

A bright smile bloomed on her face as she turned. "Good morning! I was beginning to wonder if you'd sleep all day, Mr. Hunter." Deftly, she poured coffee in a heavy mug and brought it over to him. "I'll have breakfast ready in about a half hour, if you want to jump into the shower."

He sipped the coffee and groaned softly. "Oh, man, that's good. I'm very tired of quick-stop grinds."

She flashed another grin over her shoulder. "So was I. That's a special Christmas blend. Very nice, I thought. I might have to find out about ordering some."

Zane shifted, gathering the blanket around his waist. He'd slept in his shorts. "To what do I owe this honor, Ms. Franklin?"

"It's not for you," she said, raising one brow. "I woke up with a yen for my own good cooking. You're just going to benefit by proximity." But even the acerbic words were edged with humor. "Go on, now, take your shower and get dressed. Nobody is allowed to eat if they aren't properly dressed."

"Yes, ma'am."

As he made his way to the bathroom, he noticed his leg was marginally better today. It was definitely too weak to hold his body weight by itself just yet, and he limped accordingly, but there was no pain except the healing pull of sore muscles. The hot shower took care of that.

In honor of her cooking, he took a minute to shave his light beard and pull his hair back out of his face, and even splashed on some scented aftershave before he joined her in the main room.

Claire lifted her head and inhaled deeply. "Mmm. Smells good."

"Not as good as it smells in here."

She gave him an impish grin. "And don't you look nice. That's what a woman likes to see when she's going to serve a meal." She gestured toward the small breakfast bar, which had been nicely set for two. A bowl of cubed, browned potatoes steamed next to a basket covered with a towel, and next to them a plate of sliced oranges. A neat pile of exquisitely browned bacon nested between salt and pepper, a jar of blueberry jam and butter. "Have a seat and get ready to feast, Mr. Hunter."

"Can't I do something to help?"

"Not a thing," she said. "I've got the eggs right here—" she dashed water into a pan on the stove and nodded to herself when it made a hot spat and evaporated "—and we can eat. Oh! If you want to get the orange juice out of the fridge, that would be okay."

He watched her pour the eggs and scramble them quickly, turning them out into a bowl with the expertise of long practice. "You really love to cook, don't you?"

"I do," she agreed, swiveling to put the eggs on the table, then swiveled back to take a bowl from beneath a lid. "The crowning touch," she said, putting a bowl of cream gravy on the already groaning table. "I make the best gravy in the country."

Zane could not remember a meal that so satisfied him. Everything was perfectly seasoned and delicately balanced. He ate with the deep, focused attention of a big man who'd been making do.

Sitting politely, but with alert ears and quivering

hindquarters, Coach also waited. Claire tossed him a bit of bacon, gone in a snap. "Well, if you'd take a little time to chew it, you could maybe enjoy it a little longer."

"You think that dog speaks English?"

"'Course he does." She held up a piece of bacon. "Coach, you want this?"

He stood up and made little movements, his eyes bright and eager. "What do you say?"

With a breathy *woof,* he lifted a paw and gave a nod, almost like a horse. "Good boy!" Claire said with a grin, and looked at Zane. "See? He understands English perfectly well."

Zane chuckled. "He's a hell of a good dog."

"He is that." She popped the last square of potato from her plate into her mouth and leaned back with satisfaction. "That was what I needed," she said with a sigh.

"Does that mean you're finished and I can have the rest of it?" Zane asked with a grin. "It's the best meal I've had in I don't know how long."

"I'm glad you enjoyed it."

"Did your mother cook like this?" he asked.

"No, I'm afraid she was not a great cook." The smile was rueful. "I worked in a café from the time I was about fourteen. That's where I learned. And I took a lot of cooking classes later. In the hotel business, you do get a chance to know some of the best chefs in the world."

Zane forced one last bite of biscuit in his mouth and realized he couldn't eat one more morsel. "You have quite a gift."

"Thanks." She got up to fetch the coffee, poured

herself a fresh cup for herself and offered it to Zane.
He nodded.

"I'll do the dishes when this has settled a bit," he
said.

"I'll let you," she replied cheerfully, then picked up
a magazine he hadn't noticed. It had a picture of a
gingerbread house on the front. "Did you ever make
one of these?" she asked.

"Sure. My mother loves that kind of stuff. Once we
made a whole castle, complete with curtain wall and
towers made of gingerbread."

"Really? That sounds like fun."

Was that envy he heard in her voice? "It was great.
We baked stained glass cookies—do you know
those?"

She shook her head, her expression intrigued. "How
do you do it?"

"I'm not sure what the basic cookie dough is. Must
be something like gingerbread, but it gets really hard.
You cut them out into shapes, like a window or a door
or something, then cut out some shape in the middle,
break up hard candy with a hammer and put the pieces
in the cutout."

"And it melts or something?"

Zane nodded. "Exactly. When you take them out of
the oven, they really look like stained glass windows.
My mother's pretty artistic, so she had all these fancy
round things, with seven different colors in the same
cookie." He sipped his coffee. "Mine were usually a
cross or something simple like that."

"She sounds great, your mother."

A faint sting of homesickness touched him as he
thought of her house the way it would be now—filled
with people almost any time of day or evening, for she

had a wide, inclusive group of friends. There would be a dozen tins of çookies on top of the refrigerator, bowls of hard candy in strategic spots— "Yeah." He inclined his head. "You'd like her. You have things in common."

"Really?" A flash of vulnerability flickered into her blue eyes.

A gentleness came over him, something so soft that he'd not felt it in years. This woman had suffered somehow, in ways she didn't want to discuss, and it made him sad. "It's hard to know how a woman will take this, so don't be offended, all right?"

A puzzled nod. "Okay."

"You're a homemaker. Not like the old fifties pearls-and-vacuum-cleaners kind of woman, but you have that gift for making a home."

"Oh!" She ducked her head and scrambled for her plate, turning away to put it in the sink. She stood there for a moment, her back to him.

Worried that he had offended her, Zane stood up awkwardly, found his balance and moved to her side. With one hand, he touched her shoulder. "Claire? I meant it as a compliment."

"I know."

He heard the unmistakable catch of tears in her words. Pierced, he ducked to catch a glimpse of her face, but she turned away farther, and even reached up to drag the cloth thing out of her hair, letting the strands fall down in a curtain that hid her even more.

"Claire," he said softly, and put his hand on her back. Then, feeling the fragility of her shoulders, he moved in close and put his body against her back, a gesture he recognized as primitively protective. He bent his head to her hair, smelling shampoo and ocean air. He rubbed her arms, so slim and strong, and without knowing he would, pressed a kiss to her crown.

And with a sudden shock, he realized he liked her. It wasn't just lust or convenience. He liked everything he'd seen—gentleness and scrappiness, bravado and vulnerability, sensuality and reserve. "I wish," he said, without knowing he would, "that there had been someone there for you, Claire."

"Don't," she whispered, bending her head away from him, her small body filling with rigid tension. "Please."

Zane recognized the protective instinct, the need to stay curled inside that hard shell, but he'd also been raised with people who hugged him. He knew when a *don't* was a *please*.

So instead of letting her go, he gently turned her around in his embrace, wrapped her body in his long arms and held her close. She held herself rigidly for a long, long moment, but when he began to stroke her hair lightly, she eased a little, then a little more, until she was leaning into him, her head tucked into his shoulder. "There's no shame in needing a hug now and then," he said into her hair.

She made a noise between a laugh and a cry, and clutched his shirt, and a burst of painful feeling went through him. Protectiveness and anger and a thousand other things.

"Why did I have to meet you like this?" she whispered, and pushed at him to lift her head. "Why now?"

Zane swallowed, recognizing that there was more than "like" mixed into that painful thud of his heart. He could love her. Soberly, he answered, "I don't know."

She raised one hand to put it on his lips. "I thought

you were too beautiful to be a good man. It doesn't usually come in the same package.''

"I'm not a good man, Claire,'' he said with regret. "Don't ever kid yourself about that.''

Her smile was sweet and regretful. "Yes, you are, Zane Hunter. I've seen enough bad guys to know.''

And if she had not said that, he might have kissed her—and that would have led to other things. But her words gave him courage to be better than he was. With a sigh, he let her go. "Why don't I get these dishes done and we'll get out for a walk? I've got to get this leg in shape.''

"Sounds good.''

The clerk at the counter in the motel office directed them to a stairway that led down a rocky face to the beach, only yards from the back of the motel. "You folks heard that the roads are closed now, haven't you?'' he added. "You want to reserve that room for the next couple of nights, too?''

Zane hid a smile. If there was no traffic in or out, it wouldn't make much difference if the room was reserved or not. "One more for sure,'' he said. "I'd really like to get out of here tomorrow morning.''

"Got plans for Christmas, do you?'' The man made a notation on a page. "Road'll be crazy on Christmas Eve, you know.''

"Not much help for it.'' He gave Claire what he hoped was a tender smile. "It's our first Christmas together. We want to spend it in Seattle.''

"Well, I'll keep my ears open for you.'' The man pursed his lips. "Truth is, they generally do get those roads open again pretty quick.''

"Good. Thanks." He paused. "Is there anyplace in town I can rent a laptop computer?"

"Sure thing." He took a business card and scribbled an address on the back. "Might want to get on over there before noon. He's closing for Christmas today."

"Thanks." Zane tucked the card in his pocket and gestured for Claire. When they stepped outside, he spied a pay phone. "I need to make a call. Do you mind waiting for a minute?"

"Is this a secret agent call?" she asked, with a glitter in her eyes. "If I find a way to eavesdrop, will I learn all kinds of neato code words?"

He chuckled. "You might. The context is the hard part."

"I figured." She gestured toward the wooden balustrade marking the edge of the cliff. "Coach and I will wait over there."

Zane dialed the codes to reach his buddy Max. He wasn't at home and Zane didn't leave a message. Max was likely at HQ, but Zane wondered if it was worth the risk to call him there. It suddenly didn't seem all that urgent. The Ghost was trapped on the other side of the swollen river. There was time to lure her out when they got to Seattle, but not until he had Claire out of the picture.

He turned away from the phone and stepped out of the breezeway where the phone was located—and stopped. Claire leaned on the wooden railing that protected walkers from the steep cliff face. Her long hair lifted on a soft ocean breeze, and she gazed out over the water with an expression of peace.

A thousand times, a million, he'd seen a woman standing in just that way. But somehow, looking at Claire, he felt winded and slightly dizzy. He stared at her, trying to pinpoint just what it was that caused the sensation, stared as she lifted her eyes to track the circling of a gull with black-tipped wings. Absently, she rubbed the top of Coach's head and said something to him, smiling when he licked her wrist.

Zane rubbed the place below his breastbone, trying to ease the ache. Then, like a boy, he broke the odd tension within him by exaggerating everything. He whistled, low and long, and when she turned, giving him a radiant smile, he tried to tell himself the warmth spreading through him was erotic longing, nothing more.

They walked along the deserted beach for a long time, only talking sporadically. Claire could tell it took a lot of effort for Zane to manage the loose sand with his weak leg, and she pretended not to notice that he was soon breathing very hard.

It worried her. Without the cast, his mobility was certainly more flexible, but the leg was a long way from being in top condition. She also suspected he was carrying a wide array of other lingering wounds from that car bomb.

When they came to a jutting cove that effectively blocked passage without a lot of climbing, Claire said, "Let's just sit here for a while. I'm not ready to go back."

Zane gave her a rueful smile. "I can see through you like cheap glass, lady." He sat on the ground and heaved a sigh. "But thanks. "

The fog had lifted a little, though it hung in streamers around the rocks and above hillocks of yellow grass. It gave Claire a delicious sense of isolation and possibility. Tossing a piece of driftwood for Coach, she commented, "I love the ocean."

"Why?"

She gave him a quizzical smile. "Don't you?"

His gaze traveled over the horizon. "Yeah. But why?"

"It's…" She breathed in the cool, damp air and gazed at the endless stretch of roiling gray, trying to isolate exactly what she responded to when she sat on a beach. "I love the sound," she said, closing her eyes to listen. Waves crashed into nearby rocks and whispered sibilantly as they ebbed and flowed over the sand. "Do you hear that?"

"It's lonely."

"Is it?" She looked at him.

He gave a mocking sigh. "That wasn't the right answer, was it."

"If it was a pickup line, it was pretty bad."

"I'll try harder." He touched her arm and rubbed it, then let his hand drop. "Go ahead. It was a serious question. Why do you love the ocean?"

"No, now I'm embarrassed. You blew it."

"I'll tell you what I like, then. The smell." He lifted his head and breathed in, and Claire found herself doing the same thing in sympathy. "That salt-and-fish smell makes me feel calm."

"Me, too." She clasped her hands around her knees. "I think what I like the best is that it's always the same. It's so huge, and vast, and deep. It's like God— always there. Always the same. Sometimes angry and destructive, but always a source of nourishment." She lifted her eyes to follow the circling of a gull, graceful and ghostly in the pearlescent glow of mist. "And beauty."

Zane stuck the end of his walking stick into the waves. "Even better—you can put your hands on the ocean."

She chuckled. "I agree."

He lifted a shoulder and gazed out over the vastness. Sitting there against the gray, he was a stark, strong mark against the land—the black hair gleaming, the cleanly chiseled lines of his face dewed like polished walnut, his shoulders broad and straight as a shelf. A twist of something powerful stirred in her chest. So beautiful, she thought, and tucked the image away in her memory.

He inclined his head. "Tell me about your mother, Claire."

Coming as it did into the unguarded moment, the question stung. "Why?"

"I think she neglected you. I think she hurt you."

"I hate to talk about her, Zane. She wasn't a bad person, really." She took in a breath of soothing ocean air. "And it's just so tawdry when I say it out loud. It sounds so whiny."

"Mmm." He nodded.

Thinking the subject had been dispensed with, Claire was surprised when he said, "I've been blabbering about my whole life. To tell you the truth, I don't do that. Maybe I want the same trust from you."

"It isn't a matter of trust. It's embarrassing. It's stupid and small and it still makes me angry."

"Does it?"

She dug a trench in the sand with one finger. "Yes." But some little nudge of something more honest made her probe the spot internally. Maybe she wasn't mad anymore.

And since her childhood had been hovering ever

since he appeared, she made a sudden decision. "Her name was Larissa," she said quietly. "She came from a hill family, real poor, and her father kicked her out when he found out she was pregnant with me. The boy didn't want anything to do with her, either, and since she turned sixteen three days after I was born, she had to do what she had to do."

"Which was?"

"A little of everything, really. Waited tables, mostly. Tended bar." Claire took a breath. "Mostly, she kept a string of men." There was an odd sense of relief in saying it out loud. "She was very attractive—very sexy—and it wasn't hard for her to keep a man around all the time." She gave Zane a twist of a smile. "Not a one was worth the gum scraped off the bottom of your shoe. She had a real talent for picking out beautiful losers."

He smiled. "I knew a woman like that, back home. Every down-and-out rodeo rider, two-bit hustler and alcoholic who ever blew through town ended up in her bed."

"That was Mama." She shook her head. "My mother could never resist doomed and beautiful in the same package. And one after the other, they got arrested or killed or just drifted off to some other town to fall deeper into the hole, and there she'd be—" She halted, realizing how much more she was spilling than she originally intended. She closed her eyes, forced herself to go on. "Crying in her beer over them."

"You loved her, didn't you?"

Claire sighed. Nodded. "I knew when I was just a little girl that I had more sense in my little finger than she had in her whole body."

"Probably because you had to take care of yourself."

"Maybe. Or maybe it's just something you're born with. It wasn't like she didn't try. When I was little, there was always a baby-sitter, usually somebody who lived close. Sometimes I went to work with her, and I liked that. Sitting there in some smoky place, watching her laugh and joke and talk to people." She shrugged. "When I got to be in about third grade, though, I was pretty much on my own. She brought me a dog—that was Jake—so I'd feel safe, some little mutt she found one night by the Dumpsters...."

She stopped and turned to face him. "Why am I telling you all this? It's stupid. Ancient history."

"Is it, Claire?" He captured a stray wisp of hair and tucked it behind her ear. "Don't you think all that shaped you?"

"Of course it did. I just don't think it has a lot of relevance." She narrowed her eyes, looked away from the compassion in his eyes. "Or maybe I don't want to think about how it shaped me."

"You've turned out fine."

"On the outside, maybe." She glanced at him, then back to the marks she was making in the sand. "I really hate myself that I can't forgive her. She's been dead for more than ten years and I'm still stomping around in my mind, glowering at her every time something comes up that I don't know that she should have taught me. Every time I see some little lost child on the news, abandoned by some clueless parent to fend for himself to eat peanut butter and crackers."

"And there you were, in your safe little tower, and I came along and ruined it."

She grinned. "Yeah, you rat."

"Sorry, kid." He winked. "I'll find a way to make it up to you."

Claire gazed at him and wanted with every cell in her body to lean over, put her hands on his face and kiss his mouth. She saw in the sudden darkening of his eyes that he would like that, too.

And both of them, at the same time, turned away.

Chapter 9

Zane set up the laptop at the kitchen bar and connected the phone to his modem. He'd sent a restless Claire out to get a cup of coffee and read a book for a while, and she'd more than happily done so. The effort of resisting the powerful sexual chemistry between them had stretched both of their nerves, and he wondered with some concern how they'd get through the evening.

As he sat on the tall stool, setting up his connections, he couldn't help wishing that this was a genuine love nest. The winter sun had finally burned off the mist, and he was distracted by the view of the cliffs and ocean visible through the window. The sun, molten gold, hung low over the sea, making a shining path toward the horizon. Admiring it, Zane wished with unexpected vehemence that he could simply step out on that golden path and walk away from everything.

But that was impossible and he knew it. Reining in

his drifting thoughts, he typed in the codes to send a beep to Max on a special pager that would allow him to know how to contact Zane. Within moments, Zane's program beeped. He opened a secured, private line and greeted his longtime friend. *Greetings, Max,* Zane typed. *Any news?*

Very interesting news. I think you will be pleased.

Can you fax it to this address?

Done. Anything else?

Yeah. I need a safe house for the woman, tomorrow or Christmas morning, depending on events. Can you set it up through HQ under some pretext? They won't give me any help till I come in.

Correct. The cursor blinked for a moment, and Zane waited. *Christmas morning is doable. Where can I contact you?*

Leave the vitals at the… He paused for a moment, wishing Claire had stayed in the room, after all. She'd know a good hotel in the Seattle area. *Hell, I don't know any hotels in the area. Alphabetically first five-star?*

Done.

I owe you, Max.

Watch your back.

Zane frowned at that. Then he typed *Always,* and signed off. He shifted screens to ready the fax receiver, and in a few moments, several pages of documents began to appear on the screen, one after the other. Four dossiers on possible identities for the Ghost, along with a note from Max, scrawled in his tiny, precise handwriting with its European slant. ''Sending on secured line. Murmurs of internal trouble over this, and pressure from external organizations. M.''

Ah. That made the caution make sense.

With a frown, Zane clicked off the connections and carried the laptop over to the couch where he could prop up his aching leg as he reviewed the documents. Each dossier was several pages long and included photographs, birthplace, arrest records, habits, known kills.

It surprised him there were four women, much less four French women, who were assassins. There turned out to be a single connection between all four—an elusive assassin named Henrique DeVilliers, who'd finally been killed in a raid on an Algerian town in the early eighties. All the women came from the same section of Paris.

His protégés, no doubt.

Zane immediately crossed one woman off his list. By her vital statistics, he saw she was too tall and probably too heavy to fit the profile of his quarry. Another had been missing since an explosion on a yacht three years before, and it was assumed she was dead.

That left two possibilities. Zane put the dossiers side by side, got out a pen and started making notes. By evening, he would know.

In an elegant room in Tacoma, Washington's finest hotel, the Ghost picked up the ringing phone. "A fax went out this afternoon," a voice at the other end of the line said without preamble.

"Yes?" She tried to keep the urgency from her voice, and the word came out harshly.

"Dossiers. Yours among them."

She swore in French, most colorfully. "Max Azul, I suppose."

"Yes."

"Where did it go?"

The informant gave her a telephone number and location. "Still behind the water line. He is not moving, not yet."

"But he will." She closed her eyes, willing herself to force frustration away. Already, she had made too many mistakes with Hunter. "Anything else?"

"Not at the moment." The informant chuckled. "Max is pretty busy on something, however. I expect I'll have more information for you in an hour or two."

"Good."

"I expect payment in the usual way." The voice went husky, suggestive.

She rolled her eyes. The fool. Men thought only with their privates. *"Mais, oui,"* she cooed in her most cultivated tone. "We'll celebrate together."

She hung up. Frustrated, she lit a French cigarette and stared out the window at the gray skies. A knot of frustration wound tighter and tighter with every delay. It made her want to scream.

But haste only made waste. She had learned that lesson well. A good assassin was more patient than a tiger. She was a very good tiger.

Impatiently, she smashed the cigarette down in the ashtray. Since there was nothing else to be done, she called for a massage and a facial. Perhaps they would send a boy this time. It was so much more amusing that way.

"We can't just sit here all night," Claire said. She heard the petulance in her voice and tried to quell it. But there, long limbed and gorgeous, sat Zane, as tempting as cherries jubilee. With impatience, she added, "I'm bored out of my mind."

"What are the alternatives?" Zane barely looked up

from the computer monitor he'd been staring at for more than an hour.

"I don't know," Claire said impatiently. "Surely they have a movie theater, or we can go out and get a margarita somewhere."

"You want to go to a movie?" He sounded puzzled. Still not with her.

Claire sighed. "No, not necessarily. Just…something. I'm not used to having nothing to do. I can't even clean in this place."

Finally, he seemed to pay attention. "We only have tonight to get through, Claire. I made arrangements to have you transported to a safe house tomorrow."

An unaccountable sense of disappointment pricked her. "Oh. Will I get to go home then?"

"I don't know. By the weekend, it should be over, but I'm not going to take any chances with your safety."

"Well," she said, "that takes care of tomorrow and the next day, but we're still looking at a long, boring evening here tonight. Let's see what's going on. Ask the man in the office."

"No." He shut the laptop and looked at her. "It isn't safe."

"We walked all over today."

"Yeah. We did. I'm just not comfortable with going out tonight. Better safe than sorry."

She sighed. "What, then?"

A wicked gleam lit his eyes, and before he could say it, Claire held up her hand. "Don't even say it." Like she needed him to say it. Like she'd been thinking about anything else all day but his mouth, which she had experienced and wanted to know better, and his hands, which had been so delectably sensual on her body last night, and promised even greater pleasure if she'd grant him more freedom of movement.

But her thinking didn't stop with what she *knew*. No sirreee, Bob. She had discovered her imagination could go places she never dreamed of. She'd found herself daydreaming about the way his belly looked this morning when he got up, the flesh the texture of buttery leather. Which led to speculations about—

Enough. She felt like she was drowning in desire. But the truth was, she had genuinely become attached to him. She liked him. She enjoyed his company. His wry humor and his easy chuckle and his genuine kindness. If she let herself sleep with him now, her heart would be shattered in a million pieces when he moved on.

And he would move on. There had been an uncomfortable echo in her heart when she spoke of her mother this morning. ''Doomed and beautiful'' didn't fit just her mother's long string of lost loves. It described Zane Hunter perfectly.

Impatiently, she snapped, ''We need to think of something else.''

''Okay, okay. Let me think.''

He leaned back, putting his head against the wall. His hair was loose, falling in a wash of heavy black silk over the back of the couch and over one shoulder. Glorious hair. She wanted to stroke it. Wash it and brush it and feel it falling over her face and breasts—

She sighed and crossed her arms, forcing herself to look away. The magazine she had purchased that morning caught the edge of her vision and she tugged it over as a distraction. ''Hey! I have an idea.''

''Let's hear it.''

She waved the magazine. "Let's make a gingerbread house."

His nose wrinkled in typical male rejection of domestic pursuits. "Nah. That's corny."

"Do you have a better idea?"

He narrowed his eyes on the ceiling, as if looking for help from some protector. "No," he finally admitted.

"Good. They have directions right here."

"I don't know. It's a lot of work for one night."

She widened her eyes. "Going somewhere?"

When he grinned, she knew she'd won. "Get your shoes on. We have to go to the grocery store. That is, if you think it's safe to go to the grocery store."

He nodded.

Outside, he asked, "Will you let me try driving? It would be a good test."

She tossed him the keys. "If you wreck it, you die. Pretty simple rules." Climbing into the passenger seat, she asked, "Did you get some important information this afternoon?"

Zane settled and adjusted mirrors and his seat. "I think so."

"Does that mean you have more of a plan?"

"Yes." He pulled out smoothly, stepped on the brake a little too hard. "Sorry."

"What are you going to do?"

"I can't give you details—"

"Of course not."

"The general plan is to get you to a safe house in Seattle, then lure the Ghost out."

"How can you do that?"

"Credit cards. I'll use one in an identity she'll recognize, and she'll take it as a signal."

A strange sense of doom rolled in her stomach. "Then what? You guys just shoot it out until one or the other of you is dead?"

He glanced at her. Shrugged and shifted, pulling smoothly into the parking lot of the grocery store. "More or less."

When he parked, Claire didn't move. "How will I ever know which of you won?"

His expression was sober. "I'll give a friend of mine instructions to inform you. Max."

In silence she absorbed the finality of the statement. "Thank you." She got out of the car. "Let's forget all this now. You can teach me a new tradition."

As they baked and cut and built and decorated, Claire covertly watched Zane. In spite of his protestations, she could tell he was enjoying himself. Cheerfully fitting together the sides of the house with stiff frosting, he mockingly said, "This is the manly part of the job."

Dryly, Claire said, "I couldn't have done it without you."

A little later, he made scallops of green to represent bushes. "If you ever tell a soul I did this, I'm afraid I'll have to have you killed."

She laughed. "Why are guys so worried about their image? I can tell you're enjoying yourself. Why not just admit it, and let some other poor slob enjoy himself, too?"

He gave her a mocking grimace. "And next I suppose you'll be wanting me to admit I like chick flicks."

"Do you?"

"No way, babe," he said in a growling voice. "Ain't no firepower, it ain't my thing." Then he stood back, his dark hands covered with drips of white and green and red frosting, to admire his bushes. From a bowl on the counter, he took some tiny cinnamon candies and stuck them, one at a time, to the green.

"I'd think you'd get enough firepower junk at work," she said.

"No way." With a wide grin, he popped some candy in his mouth. "You know how cool I am when I know that they made a mistake in firepower?" With a click of his tongue, he added, "Only downside is, I can't tell anybody."

"A true masculine dilemma." She sprinkled red sugar over the marshmallow fluff on the "ground" around the house to make a path to the front door.

Next to her, Zane started whistling "Here We Come A-Wassailing," and she smiled. Who was he, really? She'd always imagined that anyone involved in espionage would have a dark outlook, would grimly have his guard up at all times. She could sense his cautiousness most of the time, and she knew that he could move as fast as necessary at split-second notice. His alertness was like that of a watchful jaguar.

Yes. Exactly like a cat. His body had a lithe grace that suggested the quick reflexes she'd seen in action more than once. And his triangular face, broad at the cheekbone, narrow at the chin, with the faint tilt at the corners of his green eyes. Even that hair, so sleek and black, made her think of a jaguar's beautiful fur, shining in the light.

And like that big cat, he could play and tease and purr—oh, yes, he could definitely purr, she was sure of it—but he could also turn instantly deadly if the need arose. Deadly without regret.

She finished the sugar and started planting gumdrops

along the path. Which was the real man? Which side showed his true nature? Was he a spy or a lover?

"Hey, Claire," he said with a hint of amusement, "would you like me to find a protractor so you could get a little more exact in your layout?"

She chuckled, looking at the precision with which she'd placed the gumdrops, in exact alignment with one another. "Please," she said, tongue-in-cheek. "Anything worth doing is worth doing well."

He licked frosting from his fingers and wiggled his eyebrows lasciviously. "A woman after my own heart."

She waved that away and went back to her gumdrops. She bet he did everything well. Very well.

Heaving a mental sigh, she returned to her musings. He was, quite probably, both a lover and a spy. Just because he didn't fit the stereotype gleaned from the movies didn't mean he wasn't the real thing. Her only mistake would be casting him as father-and-husband material.

But it was very tempting. She doubted she'd ever met a man who had so many of the right qualifications. Intelligent, good-natured, easy in the sound of his own laughter, but also strong willed. A man who could dispense a hug to an inarticulate, wounded woman, a man who could fix the mistakes on a Christmas tree and be cajoled into building a gingerbread house, had a lot more emotional depth than the usual run of male.

"Don't, Claire," he said.

She started guiltily, caught in the act of staring at him with a stupid, sentimental smile on her face. "Don't what?" she asked, a flush of guilt creeping up her neck.

He shook his head, his face very sober. "Don't look

at me with that hero crap in your eyes. It's not true. I can be decent when the need arises, but it would be a mistake to think any of this is the real me."

Which was exactly what she'd been thinking, and yet she couldn't help protesting, "You are too hard on yourself."

"No." Carefully, he put down the candy in his hand and went to the sink to wash away the icing. "I'm a realist. I agreed to this charade because I am basically a gentleman and I can see you aren't the kind of woman who will handle casual sex very well, which would be my usual choice of activity when stranded with a good-looking woman for a space of time."

The embarrassment crawled up to her ears.

He turned off the water with more force than necessary and grabbed a towel, drying his fingers with brutal efficiency. She watched his hands to avoid his eyes, which had hardened to a cold, sharp emerald. "And that's what it would be, Claire, casual. Wham, bam, thank you, ma'am. I'm just like all those guys your mother found to keep her warm at night, a doomed man who never really got the right answers and finds himself too old and too entrenched to change his tricks now."

"Zane—"

He stepped up and took her chin in fingers that were not particularly gentle. "Do you know how many people I've killed? And what's worse, how little it even means to me?"

He held her chin at an angle, forcing her to look into his face. Her heart pounded too hard in her chest at the sudden appearance of the killer she had just admitted must live within him, but she still found herself noticing that his lashes were extraordinarily long and black, which was what gave his expression gentleness, even now. An accident of nature.

"I don't care," she said.

"You should."

His jaw hardened and his fingers were nearly bruising, but Claire recognized in a flash that it was an attempt to put her at arm's length, that while his mouth and his hard grip were saying one thing, his eyes were no longer cold and glittery but full of a kind of haunted pain he'd kept very well hidden till this moment.

Very carefully, she reached up and wrapped her fingers around his hand, and took it away. "I told you, I've seen bad. And you aren't it." A swell of something strong and right moved through her, an exhilarated sense of faith she could not remember ever feeling, not once, in all her life. She pressed a kiss to his palm. "Whatever demons are haunting you—and I do believe they're causing you pain—you are a good man."

Before he could protest again, she slipped by him, headed for her bedroom, only turning at the door. "You're right about one thing. I'm not the kind of woman who can handle recreational sex. Frankly, I find it a loathsome perversity. So, I'll say good night and spare you having to act out of character any longer."

He kept his head bowed, and his voice was rough. "Good night, Claire."

Zane didn't move for long moments after he heard the door click shut behind her. He didn't move because he was afraid of storming after her, pushing past all her barriers and showing her what a bastard he really could be. At the center of his palm, the same palm that remembered the erotic feel of her aroused nipple trailing along the love line, he felt the imprint of her gentle, shattering kiss.

Eventually, he picked up the knives scattered over the counter, and the bowls, now empty, that had held candy and various colors of frosting. He ran a sink full of sudsy, hot water and washed everything with methodical, thoughtless efficiency.

There was a roar in his head, a building storm that was knocking him off-kilter. Out of step. Out of his head. As he swept stray crumbs into his damp palm, his vision was filled with the sight of her honey-colored hair falling down to cover her face this morning. Sweeping the floor with a rather abused broom, he thought of her face, shuttered and somehow still vulnerable, dewed with mist as they walked along the beach.

His chest hurt when he thought of her wide, bright blue eyes looking into his with such utter faith, without a hint of cynicism or self-preservation or doubt. A faith he didn't deserve. A faith that was all the more shattering because he knew she had rarely bestowed it on anyone.

In despair, he slumped on the couch. Tomorrow, he would set her free. Maybe she could go on believing in him that way. Maybe he wouldn't have to see that shining belief dimmed, first to suspicion, then to distrust, and finally, hate.

She would hate him in the end. Because he really was not the man she thought she saw. Once, he might have been. Once, he might have deserved that faith, even welcomed it.

But that man had died, on a gilded street in Paris when he'd vowed revenge—not for the good of the world, but for himself.

A bitterness rose in his mouth. Once, he, too, had believed. Not anymore.

In the quiet, he must have finally fallen into a doze. When he started awake, the light still burned in the kitchen, and his first thought was that he'd been a fool to leave it on. It made him a perfect mark from outside.

He was definitely slipping.

Intently, he listened to the near-roar of silence in the heart of the night. Nothing…then a faint whimper.

Claire.

He jumped to his feet, and in spite of the jolt of pain that went through his leg at the sudden movement, he moved to her door and carefully turned the handle.

Coach, evidently undisturbed by the cries coming from his mistress, lifted his head when Zane peered into the darkness. He lay on the floor at the foot of the bed, and his tail wagged as Zane slid around the door and padded into the room.

On the bed, Claire was curled tight around a pillow and made not a single move, while the soft, protesting cries came out of her, almost against her will. There was terrible fear in the sound, the fear of a child.

For one long moment, he simply stood there, winded and furious at both her mother, for not caring for her child properly, and at himself, for insisting upon knowing her sad history when she'd plainly put it behind her. He was responsible for this bad dream, for both shattering the peace of the world she'd built, stone by stone, and for dredging up bad memories this morning.

And then, although he knew it was the wrong move, that he would be sorry, he moved into the room, and lifted the covers and crawled in beside her. It wasn't like he was coming on to her, he reasoned. He still wore his jeans and his shirt and his socks. He was only offering comfort.

He moved close and gathered her small body close to his large one, making a cove in which she could take refuge. She startled, pushing madly at him, and he stroked her hair. "Shh," he whispered. "It's just me. You're safe. I have you. Go to sleep."

And she curled close, her head on his shoulder, her arms crossed in front of her, even her knees drawn up, and Zane simply held her while she slept, making sure she was safe, wishing he could drive the demons away.

He did not sleep, and it wasn't, as he might have expected, a sense of arousal that kept him awake. Her body felt infinitely precious next to him, her shoulders almost heartbreakingly slim and roped with muscle, her back lean and strong. And her hair, silky and smelling of sugar, brushed his face. A part of him responded, wanted to weigh the plumpness of breast and the round of her bottom, but it was enough to simply feel her close, hold her.

And somehow, holding her made him remember her hotel. The homey warmth. The smell in the air. The hearty soup. He remembered the smell of starch in the bedcovers and the thick towels and the artful, warm details in every small thing. Out of nothing, she'd created a home, not only for herself and for the child she'd been, but for any weary traveler, anyone seeking rest and comfort.

He hated that he'd torn her from that safe, warm world. Hated himself for dragging her into his mess.

In the long, sleepless time, he realized there was one thing he could do for Claire Franklin. One thing to make up for what he'd stolen, the one thing he had that she did not.

One small thing.

Chapter 10

The scent of man seeped into Claire's dream world. She stirred a little, wondering how she knew it was male, and in her dream she chuckled as images of after-shave bottles, and the smooth brown neck of Zane Hunter passed through her mind. In her dream, she sighed with happiness and nuzzled close to that neck, inhaling deeply, brushing her lips over his throat.

A hand fell on her hair and she arched into it, amazed at the size and strength of it over her scalp. The warmth.

"Claire?"

With a jerk, she awakened to discover the dream was real. The neck under her lips was warm; the flesh was smooth and smelled of forest and male. Confused and shocked, she tried to push away.

His embrace tightened. "Take it easy," he whispered. She felt the warmth of his breath sough over the part in her hair, and it sent a jolt of arousal swirling down her spine. The roughness of denim shifted beneath her bare knee and the point of his collar pressed into her cheek. He was dressed. That much was good. She moved a little, and felt fabric slide over her back. She was dressed, too, then.

Whew.

But dressed was a relative term. Dressed, in her case, was a worn-thin T-shirt that left her breasts free to press against the length of his ribs, and a pair of tiny panties that left her legs bare as they tangled against his jeans-clad thighs. Realizing this, she made a move to pull away, but Zane caught her knee in the vise of his legs. At the same moment, his left hand moved on her back in a firm circle, the gesture somehow carrying with it a wealth of desire and restraint.

"Don't go just yet," he said, his voice hushed.

Claire told herself to resist, but even as she formulated the cautionary statement, that wild creature that had sprung free in her that first night, in front of the Christmas tree, sailed free. It fluttered madly in the cage of her ribs, and the thrilling intensity of it silenced the voice of reason.

She closed her eyes and let the swell of hunger fill her. Slowly, she moved her nose against his neck and unfurled her hand to gauge the contours of his chest. Zane stirred gently, his hand moving on her back, shoulder to shoulder, down the spine, up into her hair.

"Ah, Claire," he said, and she heard it through his chest. "You're too good for me, you know."

She rose on her arm. "Am I?" she asked softly, and drew a hand down his face. His deep, starry eyes were sober, his mouth very still. Caught in something beyond herself, she touched his mouth with her fingers, watched his eyes close as he resisted, felt his hand tighten on the small of her back. "I don't think so, Zane."

She bent her head, letting her hair fall around them, and kissed him. And on his lips, she tasted nights full of stars and foggy beaches. She tasted honor and despair and a narcotic promise of pleasure. A pulse of light moved through her, and she eased her body down against his, welcoming the solidity of him, the tensile strength in his arms and chest.

He made a low noise and laced a hand through her hair and kissed her back, but gently, accepting whatever she gave without demands of his own. She kissed his jaw, and his cheekbone, and stretched a little to reach his broad, high forehead, then skimmed down the blade of a nose, back to his mouth.

"Claire," he protested. His breath whispered against her lips.

"Shh," she said, letting her lips whisper over his. She moved her hand on his chest, down to his stomach, and pushed up the shirt to touch his flat, brown belly. It felt both harder and softer than she had imagined, for his skin was silken and supple, the texture of very fine doeskin, and below that flesh was muscle that was nearly as ungiving as bone. It surprised her a little, that powerful feeling of muscle. She had not realized he would be so strong. She bent her head and kissed him there, on the plane of his café au lait belly, making a circle with her mouth, pushing up his shirt so she could kiss his ribs. "I've been wanting to do this for days," she said.

With a sound of need pushing past his boundaries, a small roar, he half sat and swiveled over her, pushing her down on the pillows to kiss her, roughly and deeply, his big hand cradling her head. The intensity of his need humbled her, and his sensual mouth sent a pulsing through her blood, and when he moved, sliding his big hand down to cover her breast, she cried out and laced a leg around his back, pulling him closer.

Together they moved restlessly, legs and arms and mouths entwined. He captured her hand and their arms met, palm to palm, wrist to wrist, and Claire wanted to cry out with the pleasure of feeling his inner arm against her own, but found she could drink of his mouth instead, drink deeply, as hungrily as she wished, and he was there, meeting that need with his own. He thrust his hips close against hers, and she arched against him, straining for the rigid flesh that rubbed against her hipbone. He bent his head to her breast, taking it into his mouth through the cloth, and she actually cried out at the sensation.

Suddenly, he paused and swore, dropping his forehead into the curve of her neck. "Damn." Breathing hard, he lifted his head. "I don't have a condom."

His eyes were luminous, and his hair was an untamed black fall around his face. For one wild moment, caught in her desire, Claire felt poised to cry, *I don't care.*

But in time she remembered that she did. "Damn."

He kissed her, very sweetly, very gently, and she felt trembling in his arms. With a soft cry, she put her arms around his shoulders and pulled him to her, burying her face in the warm curve of his shoulder. A sigh escaped him as he let himself be embraced. The muscles under her arms relaxed, and he rubbed his cheek against hers, a gesture both erotic and tender.

And in that instant, Claire understood that she was lost. He felt right in her arms, fitting the spaces, and his smell was one she'd been waiting for. And in the tender restraint and protestations of his true self—protestations he made to push her away—she saw honor.

A wave of pure emotion washed through her, stunning and powerful, and she tightened her hold, yearning to breathe him into her body somehow, amazed at how precious he felt against her. As if he felt the same strange wave, he gathered her closer, closer, until it seemed they might truly meld.

After a long moment, he lifted his head. "Will you stay with me one more night, Claire?"

She looked at him without speaking, seeing that he offered only tonight, nothing more than that. "Yes," she whispered. The only possible answer.

"It's Christmas Eve. You don't mind?"

There was, in his eyes, more Christmas than she'd ever seen. She pulled a hand free and reached up to his hair, twining the strands around her wrist before she answered. "I don't mind."

A flicker of something akin to pain crossed his face, and he kissed her once more, fiercely. "Thank you."

When Claire disappeared into the bathroom to freshen up, Zane flipped on the television to check out the weather and learned that the roads had been reopened sometime in the middle of the night. Claire, dressed down to her sneakered feet, came out to hear the last of the news report. In the film clips, they showed cars passing debris and thick mud spilled over the tarmac, but it would be quite passable in her sports utility vehicle. "I'm glad I have my truck," she commented.

"Yeah. Definitely a stroke of luck." Zane stood, clicking off the television and tossing the remote down on the coffee table. "Let's get out of here."

Claire looked around at the tiny cabin and the pretty

view through the windows and the cheery little Christmas tree. "Why can't we just stay here one more night? It's cozy."

That shuttered expression crossed his face, telling her that he knew more than he was saying. "I know. But we've been here too long. Better to keep moving."

"Oh." She glanced away. Nodded.

"I made some coffee." He gestured toward the counter. "We'll stop on the road and get some breakfast when we get by the flooded areas."

"Okay." She poured coffee, feeling a little awkward. It had been one thing to wake up and somehow drift into the intimacy of his embrace; it was quite another to look at him now, his hair pulled back, his mask of businesslike efficiency not quite able to hide his weariness as he limped from one part of the room to another. "How is your leg feeling this morning?" she asked.

One shoulder lifted. "All right."

She hesitated. "Zane, have you considered the possibility of letting someone else bring this assassin in?"

"No." The answer was instantaneous. He raised cold green eyes to her face. "It's something I have to do."

But he was tired. He wasn't so young anymore. It made her feel sick to imagine what might happen to him out there. "What if she kills you?"

A faint bitterness tightened his mouth. "Then she wins."

And in the words, Claire heard that he expected to lose—or at least considered it a very strong possibility. It made her heart stutter, and she bent her head to her coffee, burning her lips when she gulped it too fast.

"I'll understand if you want me to take you to a safe house today instead of spending the night with me."

Everything was in that sentence. He was telling her that he was very likely doomed, that he really had nothing to offer her at all—not even the kind of nothing her mother's boyfriends had had. She lifted her eyes and took in the soberness of his face, then swallowed the lump in her throat so she could speak. "I have to think about it."

"I understand." He turned back to his packing. She saw him tuck the big black gun into the back of his jeans. Casually. Without thought.

She was in way over her head. How could she have been spinning such wild fantasies about this man? She'd seen the bullet holes in her living room. She'd heard the pings of bullets hitting her car. She'd seen the scars on his body.

But it just hadn't been real. Not until he tucked that big black gun into the back of his jeans.

At an ATM in town, Zane drew out a sizable amount of cash on one of his credit cards, explaining to Claire that it wouldn't matter if the Ghost knew they had been in the small town now that they were leaving. Claire made a little joke about the intricacies of spy stuff, but couldn't shake the sense of danger the comment brought home.

Was the Ghost in Seattle, waiting?

Aside from crossing the flooded river that still ran too high for Claire's tastes, the drive was uneventful. The clouds and wet had cleared off, leaving a sparkling blue sky embroidered at the edges with vistas of mountains in shades of dark blue and crisp white. As they passed Tacoma, the Sound glittered in oceanic splendor, dotted with white ferries.

They had spoken little on the drive, each absorbed in their own thoughts, but Claire felt a sense of peace at the familiarity of the Sound. Quietly, she said, "It's so beautiful."

"Yeah, it is."

He shifted on the seat, and she wondered if his leg was hurting. She suspected it was.

"Can you see your island from here?" he asked.

"Barely." She pointed. "Look right between those breaks."

"Home sweet home."

"Yes." A wave of longing shook her. She ached to walk up those steps, to water her plants and make beds. "I'm looking forward to getting back."

"I bet."

She glanced at him. "Where's home for you, Zane?"

"Nowhere, really. Wherever I hang my hat."

"Really? You don't have an apartment somewhere, a room you keep, anything like that?"

"Well, yeah. I have a condo in Virginia, but I spend maybe three days a year there. And I have a flat in Paris."

She grinned. "'A flat in Paris.' That sounds so jet-set."

"It isn't. You would like it. It's old, with big long windows that look over the rooftops. A lot of sunshine for your plants." He lifted a hand, hesitated, then pushed her hair back from her face, his fingers lingering on her neck. "You like plants, don't you?"

Swallowing to dislodge the sudden swell of emotion in her throat, Claire half smiled. Lightly, she said, "Oh, yes. You should see my gardens in the summertime. Banks and banks of flowers. The garden is a favorite with my guests.'' She signaled a lane change. ''One day, maybe you can visit in June. It's prettiest then.''

''Yeah?'' One finger touched her earlobe. ''Tell me about it.''

Claire did. She described the dahlias and shrubs, telling him the color scheme he would find if he arrived in June. He listened with apparent interest, as if he somehow needed to hear about it. ''The lavender is blooming then, too,'' she added. ''It makes the air smell like perfume.''

''Sounds great.'' She had the sense that she'd somehow renewed him with her little descriptions. He stretched. ''Are there places to go camping and hunting on the islands anywhere? Do people do that around here?''

''Of course. The San Juans are popular for that kind of thing. I don't know about hunting, but definitely camping. People also rent pleasure boats and cruise the sound, which is kind of like camping.''

''Really? And who navigates the boats?''

''You can hire people to do it, or you can do it yourself. There are some excellent tours on yachts, very pricey with gourmet food and wines and all that.''

''Have you ever taken one of the cruises?''

''No. I've ridden the ferry to Vancouver a couple of times, and once down to Tacoma, but the truth is, I'm a lot happier seeing to the comfort of others than I am letting someone wait on me.''

''Why?''

She shrugged. ''Too many years in the hotel business, I guess.''

He regarded her steadily without speaking for a moment. "We'll have to work on that."

Against her will, a blush crept up her neck. Focusing on joining the increasingly heavy traffic flowing into Seattle, she gave no answer, but he laughed and reached out a hand to rub her shoulder.

Then the traffic became a serious concern and Claire had to keep her attention on the road. Zane directed her to a downtown parking garage. She drove up the twisting concrete ramps and parked in shadows, shivering as she got out.

He shouldered his pack and waited while Claire leashed Coach. "Keep the ticket close," he said. "You'll need it."

His meaning was clear: when she returned to her vehicle, she would be on her own. The knowledge pierced her. Unable to hide her dismay, she met his gaze across the hood.

"This is it, kid," he said. "Stay or go."

She tucked the ticket into her coat pocket, unable to look at him for the sudden wave of tears welling in her eyes. She pretended to be busy with adjusting the leash. With a panicky sense of irrationality, she thought she'd cried more tears in the few days since he'd walked into her life than she had in all the twenty-eight years before.

And she had a feeling there would be more before she was finished.

Struggling to unfasten the Velcro on her pocket, she started when Zane's feet appeared beside her own. "Claire," he said roughly. His hand fell on her hair.

Blindly, she moved into his embrace, pressing her face into his chest, gripping his sides fiercely. "I'm really going to miss you," she whispered. "It's crazy.

I've only known you for a few days, but I can't even imagine how it was before.''

"I know.'' His mouth touched her hair. "But you'll be back to normal life and forget all about it in no time.''

Claire, clutching him close, doubted that very much. He didn't seem in any hurry to let her go, either. His hands moved on her back, and his cheek pressed against her hair. "I guess so,'' she said at last, but made no move to release him.

"I'll take you to the safe house. You'll be protected there.''

"No,'' she said, and certainty moved in her chest. She raised her head. "No, I want to stay with you.''

His expression was unguarded for the briefest moment, and Claire saw disbelief and release and *need* cross his face before he kissed her fiercely. "Thank you,'' he breathed, and kissed her eyelids, then clasped her close to him in the same hungry, engulfing embrace he'd given this morning. Then he took her hand. "Come on.''

Out on the street, they entered the flow of foot traffic, and Claire could feel the palpable energy in the shoppers. People were generally polite in Seattle, but there was a pleasantness to the spirit this afternoon that went beyond even that. It buoyed her. "Have you ever noticed how nice people are on Christmas Eve?''

"I have.''

A woman passing them on the sidewalk did a double take when she got an eyeful of him, and when she realized Claire had caught her, the woman gave her a rueful grin that said *I can't help myself.* Claire smiled in acknowledgment.

"So what are we doing now?'' she asked.

"First, I need to get to a pay phone and do a couple of mysterious secret agent things. Then—" his fingers slid between hers "—we should find a room. Do you have a preference?"

Claire immediately thought of the aging but luxurious Vanessa Hotel. "I have a better idea. Let's get a room first, and then you can take care of your mysterious errands. There's a shopping area nearby the hotel I'm thinking of, and I could amuse myself there for a while."

"You're a shopper?"

She raised her eyebrows. "You *did* see my bed-and-breakfast, Mr. Hunter?"

"Sure." His expression insisted he had no idea what the connection was.

"One does not simply walk into the local discount or department store and discover all the best details already arranged for one's pleasure," she said in a prim voice. "If one intends to create ambience and beauty, one must always prowl any possible shop for any perfect detail that may be waiting."

He chuckled "What did you use for an excuse before you got the hotel?"

"I couldn't really indulge the habit much until I bought it. I was quite thrifty."

"No—shoppers are born, not made. You found a way."

Coach went rigid over some scent on a lamppost, and Claire tugged impatiently on the leash. "Well, as it happens, I was awfully fond of St. Vincent de Paul's. And Goodwill. And Salvation Army." She grinned.

They stopped at the corner, and without any warning at all, Zane tugged her hand and bent his head and kissed her. Right there in public. In full view of the world. A shock of pleasure and happiness made her catch his face and kiss him back exuberantly. "Every woman within sighting distance is desperately jealous of me at this moment," she said, sotto voce.

"And every man wants to toss me aside."

"Oh, I doubt that very much." Still, she was pleased. She couldn't remember anyone ever saying such an extravagantly flattering thing to her in her life.

For one moment, standing on a crowded corner with people flowing all around them, and the sound of Christmas carols in the air, and a bright winter sun warming the top of her head, Claire was purely happy. For the first time in her life, she had no interest in what the future would bring. She didn't want to think about tomorrow.

Only now.

She gazed up at him, drinking in the fine fall of his black hair, his green eyes in the angled face, his smiling mouth, and she let the knowledge of the coming night fill her with anticipation. Tonight, she would lie next to him. Tonight, she would love him. Tonight, if she wished, she could kiss every square inch of his beautiful face and form and wrap his hair around her wrists and listen to his heart and feel him—

"That's one devilish expression you have on your face, woman," he said.

"Wait until you see what's behind it." She turned away. "Come on. The light is green."

Zane followed her into the elegant old Vanessa, admiring the arched stonework and extravagant details in order to distract himself from the temptation of Claire herself. At the desk, he took charge, paying a hefty fee to get permission to take Coach up to the room, and that occupied his thoughts for another ten minutes.

But then he had the keys in his hand and they turned toward the elevators, crossing a luxurious, Arabian-style red carpet between banks of overstuffed chairs.

Before now, he'd been attracted to her. He'd liked her spirit and strength, and her beautiful rear end, from the start. He'd come to love the flash of her bright blue eyes and the toss of her head. He'd felt a dizzying array of things in the few days since they'd met: protective and aroused and frustrated and even angry. He'd been beguiled and bewildered and touched.

But today, there was such light around her that it made all the other things he'd felt fade to insignificance. Light seemed to pour from her skin. It glittered like stars in her eyes and rippled from the gloss in her hair, swinging free on her shoulders. Everything about her made him feel faintly dizzy with wonder—the robust sound of her laughter, the rosy color of her lips, the brush of her index finger over his palm, the shape of her jaw.

He'd known dozens of women in his time. He'd fallen in love with one or two of them. But he couldn't remember ever feeling this sense of enchantment before. He ached to make love to her, but conversely, wanted to wait, drawing out the anticipation as long as possible. He wanted to shower her with gifts and protect her from harm and kill any other man she so much as smiled at.

Bemused by his reaction, he paused at the elevators. "Why don't you go on up? I'll get my business taken care of and meet you here in a couple of hours."

"You don't even want to come up for a minute?"

He picked up her hand and kissed the palm. "It

wouldn't be just a minute," he said roughly. "And I'm still without protection."

That delectable heat blossomed in her eyes and she smiled. "A couple of hours, then." She lifted on her toes and pressed a kiss to his mouth. "Don't keep me waiting too long."

"No," he said, and the word was a promise.

Back out in the day, he paused a moment on the sidewalk, aware of a preternaturally heightened sense of awareness. Colors seemed more intense. Sounds were more acute. He could smell everything, every tiny note in the air—the hint of cinnamon from some nearby shop, a scent of frying doughnuts, the more prosaic city odors of oil and gasoline fumes. He wasn't sure what caused the awareness. Maybe it was as simple as knowing he might not have much time to enjoy it. Maybe it was Claire.

Maybe, he thought with a grin, he was just losing his mind. Not so bad, if it came on a man like this.

There was business he needed to take care of, however, and bemusement, however pleasant, would not get it done. He hailed a cab and gave the driver an address on the other side of the city, which he'd looked up in the phone book. Once there, he made his first call, to the alphabetically first hotel on the list, and the front desk clerk who answered assured him there was a package there for him. It was several miles away; he promised he'd pick it up in a couple of hours.

Next he called Max, who answered immediately. Briefly, he let him know all was well, and that he would deliver Claire to the safe house the following day. "You have arrived in Seattle?" Max asked.

"Yeah, we're here."

A brief but pregnant pause met his words. "Ah. I

see,'' Max said. ''Shall I meet you there tomorrow, then?''

''Yeah. We'll go from there.''

''Very good.'' Max paused. ''Happy Christmas, my friend.''

''Same to you, Max.''

Zane hung up, and whistling at the sense of freedom he felt, he set out for the rest of his errands.

Chapter 11

The Vanessa was old and gracious, and had long been one of Claire's favorites. The room they were given more than met her expectations. A rug in cranberry and blue and cream, boasting an elegant pattern of cabbage roses, covered the floor, and the overstuffed chairs were upholstered in single notes to accent the rich colors. A rolltop desk and sideboard took up one wall; a mahogany table sat beneath a pair of long windows, draped in light, airy fabrics, and the bed was an excellent imitation of an antique four-poster. The hotelier in her was pleased by the small touches—loofah sponges on the claw-footed bathtub, a collection of crystal water and wineglasses on the sideboard; fresh purple and white freesias in a vase on the table. Very nice.

Coach paced the room and settled in one corner, happy after the long walk. She ordered coffee and sandwiches from room service, and fed him roast beef with water served in the sparkling clean plastic trash can from the bathroom.

The windows looked out toward the west, and a bank of thick clouds were moving in over the city. For some reason, the sight made her heart lift. Snow on Christmas Eve struck her as deeply romantic.

Romantic. She smiled. It was a romantic room, as she'd known it would be. It felt homey, too, unlike one in a chain hotel, and she suspected Zane was feeling a little homesick over the holiday. She wondered what she could do to make it less lonely for him, and with that in mind, she went out to shop.

She meandered among the stores, picking out little things to put in a stocking for him—a bag of gold coins, a giant candy cane, jelly beans, a gorgeous apple she bought from a produce stand. In a rock shop, she found a turtle, no more than five inches long, carved beautifully out of a green stone that made her think of the color of Zane's eyes. It sat on the counter as if it had been waiting for her, and as she held it in her hand, a dozen flashes of memory danced over her vision—his rueful smile on the ferry that morning, telling her about "turtle stories," the starriness of his long eyelashes as he slept, the fierceness of his mouth when he'd held the gun in his hand.

"Must be for someone very special," the man behind the counter said.

"What?" Claire looked up, shaken from her reverie.

"The turtle," he said. "Must be for someone very special, judging by that smile on your face."

"Yes," she said. "He is."

By the time she ducked out of the shop, a cold wind had started to blow. She and Coach hurried back to the hotel, ducking into the lobby with gratitude. Coach

shook himself vigorously and airy bits of dog hair flew
into the air, littering the beautiful carpet.

Naturally, the concierge saw everything. Claire gave
him an apologetic little smile. He gestured her over,
and Claire went, trying to think of an apology that
would work on the thin-lipped young man. "Sorry,"
she said. "He's just being a dog."

"Oh, no harm done!" He gave her an envelope and
winked. "Your husband asked me to give you this."

"Thank you," she said, breathless from the rush in
the cold. Walking toward the elevator, she turned the
envelope over and opened the flap. A simple card was
enclosed.

A few more errands left to run, but I've made
reservations for dinner at seven and will pick you
up then. I chose a dress I thought you would like.
                                                     Zane

She was a little disappointed, but his absence would
give her a chance to hang his stocking. Maybe take a
nice, long, hot bath in the huge tub and listen to music.
She would wash her hair and shave her legs, and then,
tonight—

A pulse jumped in her throat. Yes. Tonight.

His pack leaned against the wall, and seeing the familiar nylon bag, Claire was relieved on some deeper
level. Had she believed he would just leave her, disappear into Seattle?

Maybe.

The dress was hung neatly in the closet. Claire
sighed in amazement when she took it out. She'd never
known a man who could choose women's clothing, but
this one could. The dress was as simple as it was ele-

gant, a knee-length black velvet, with long sleeves and a square-cut bodice. He'd bought stockings, as well, expensive silk from a department store she did not allow herself to enter, and a pair of black sandals in two sizes. The smaller one fit perfectly.

Holding the dress up to herself, she laughed at her reflection. "I think I've fallen into a movie," she said to Coach, who cocked his ears. "Who is this guy, anyway?"

But she knew. She knew very well. It had only been four days, but she'd spent every minute of that time with him. A faint voice said that it wasn't real time. It was dream time, and had no bearing on the rest of her life. The voice said it as a warning, but Claire suddenly didn't care.

This time with Zane *was* a dream. She would eventually wake up, return to her world and continue with life the way it had been. She would make soup and plant dahlias and hum under her breath as she made beds. Her life would return to normal.

But she would never be the same.

Hanging the dress back in the closet, she kicked off her shoes, then she went into the bathroom and turned on the taps, humming under her breath as she poured bath salts into the water. She tied up her hair, looking at herself in the mirror. It was the same face she'd seen for twenty-eight years. The same arms, the same breasts, the same hair.

And yet, something in her was changed. Frowning at her reflection, she wondered if she was suffering a form of "hostage mentality." Had she lost perspective these past few days out of a need to survive? Had she cast Zane Hunter in the role of hero because the alternative was too threatening?

She had a deep need to be safe. She knew that. She'd gone to great lengths as a child to create a sense of safety where none truly existed. An eight-year-old girl should never have been spending her nights alone, but Claire had eaten her canned ravioli and watched television and brushed her teeth and taken baths and gone to bed on time because it made her feel safe. And she had taken her dog into her bed to hang on to because it made the world safe.

But it wasn't safety she felt now. She felt exhilarated and threatened and eager. She was filled with a giddy kind of anticipation she'd never known when she imagined how it would be to sleep in his arms. She felt strangely as if she was about to be married, and tonight was the honeymoon, and maybe her groom was a soldier, shipping out in the morning.

"Come on, Claire," she said. "At least be truthful."

And because the only person she'd ever really had was herself, she met her own blue eyes frankly in the mirror and said, "I'm in love with him. And nothing else really matters right now."

Her reflection fleetingly looked stricken, but the smile was true and honest. Good enough.

In a hotel room across town, Simone picked up the ringing phone.

"Hunter has a date at a safe house tomorrow," her informant said. "He's going to deliver the woman there."

At last. "Very good."

"When will I get my reward?"

"When he is dead, *chéri*. When he is dead." She hung up before he could protest. From her wide windows, she viewed the glittering Sound, and wondered if the game might be ended more quickly than tomorrow. Perhaps one or the other had slipped up.

On a hunch, she sat down at her laptop and called up Claire Franklin's credit cards. Methodically, she scanned records going back ten years, seeking only one city: Seattle. Surely, if the woman had settled in the area, she'd made a trip in the past. Where had she stayed?

The list was dismayingly long. It looked as if Franklin had spent a good deal of time in Seattle two years ago, probably while she'd been shopping and making deals for the bed-and-breakfast on the island. Most of that time had been spent in a business hotel that boasted suites. Simone would check it, but her instincts said it was the wrong call.

An hour later, she had to admit defeat. Frustrated, she clicked off the computer and lit a cigarette. Her nerves were coiled tight as springs, and she rolled her head, wishing for her Arabian lover—not the white-fleshed double agent at the Organization. She thought of Jamal's hands, gliding over her body, rolling the tension from her neck, and her head suddenly popped up.

If Hunter was in Seattle, why had he not delivered the woman to the safe house by now? Had her informant's information been incorrect, or—she narrowed her eyes thunderously—had his duplicity been discovered?

No. He'd been undetected for more than a year, since Simone had seduced him in Frankfurt with her most elegant tricks, and she had done nothing yet to tip her hand, to let the Organization know she had an informer.

Which left the reason for Hunter's failure to deliver Franklin to a safe house to speculation—rather interesting speculation at that. The tiger smiled. A woman with more stubbornness than sense had captured Hunter's straying eye, a woman from the wrong side of the tracks, one who'd managed to save his delectable hide from the most notorious assassin in the world.

Curious, Simone quickly typed a file name and called up a photo of Franklin, taken two years before for a hotel party. Simone inclined her head. The woman was ordinary, really. Neither blond nor brunette. Pale eyes, clean features without a hint of seduction. Her figure, too, looked ordinary.

But if Hunter was careless enough to bring her to a city where he could have her safeguarded and still could not yet part with her, there was something that had captured him. The Hunter had been snared. Interesting indeed.

Simone smoothed her hands down her own form. In a Rio bar, two years before, she had spied a glorious creature, as feral and dangerous and thrilling as a—tiger—drinking gold shots of tequila in the bar. She'd nearly purred at the weight of his long black hair and the depth of his green eyes. From her arsenal of tricks, she'd pulled her very best techniques of seduction.

And found him unmoved.

Only later had she learned it was Hunter she'd tried to lure to her bed. Hunter, who had—that very evening—disarmed her assassination attempt.

She blinked long cat eyes, tapping one tooth with her finger. At last, she smiled. It had been a very big mistake for Hunter to let his heart grow vulnerable, for now the tiger coiled and would pounce, her claws raking to pieces that softest place.

And at last, her enemy would die.

*   *   *

Claire was ready when Zane's knock came at a quarter to seven. She had soaked in a hot tub scented with bath salts and scrubbed her flesh smooth with the loofah, then rubbed luxurious creams into every inch of that buffed skin. Her hair shone, and she had sent down to have someone bring her a selection of cosmetics.

As she reached for the door, it occurred to her that Zane had never seen her in full armor. She'd not even had a lipstick with her this past week. Smiling, she opened the door, a greeting on her lips.

A greeting she forgot. The man in her doorway could never be mistaken, not for three seconds, for a transient—as Claire had suspected the first time she saw him in her driveway at the bed-and-breakfast.

Gone were the jeans and boots, the baseball hat and jean jacket—and with them, the western man she thought she knew.

The man who stood in the hallway was elegant and dangerous and darkly sexy, his tall, lean form made for the Italian wool suit that framed his broad shoulders and emphasized the nip of his waist and his lean hips. His hair was combed straight back from his high forehead, and his skin showed the ministrations of a good barber. He looked dangerous and beautiful, savage and suave, and Claire could not even find a breath of air to speak.

The only thing that saved her from complete embarrassment was the stunned expression on his face, his reaction to *her* transformation. His eyes widened slightly, and his gaze touched her hair, pulled into a smooth knot at her nape, fell to the generous square of flesh visible at the bodice, then lowered to her legs in the black stockings.

They both spoke at the same moment.

"You look—"

"You are—"

Then he stepped up, took her hand and bent to place a kiss on her neck. "Claire, you are so beautiful."

She looked at him. "So are you."

His smile flashed, and beneath the polished exterior, she saw the man she had come to know. Her heart leapt a little. His name echoed in her head, *Zane, Zane, Zane,* like a magic spell.

"I have a car waiting," he said, "but first, I thought that neckline might need a little something." He pulled a box from his pocket, and she sensed a little shyness in the way he offered it. "Merry Christmas."

Claire laughed happily and tore away the paper, excited and pleased. But when she opened the box, she let go of a soft gasp. "Zane, I can't accept this."

"Yes, you can." He took the delicate chain from the box and fastened it around her neck, then stepped back. "I knew it was right. Exactly the same color as your eyes." He smiled and turned her toward the mirror. "Look."

And once again, she came face-to-face with herself. With a hand that trembled, she touched the stone, a flat oblong of lapis lazuli in an elegant frame of silver. "Thank you."

He met her gaze in the mirror. "My pleasure," he said. He touched her cheek with one hand, a suddenly sober expression on his mouth. Then he closed his eyes with a sigh and bent to kiss the edge of her shoulder. Watching that gleaming, well-groomed man bend and kiss the elegant woman in the mirror, Claire felt a powerful wave of desire. She lifted a hand to his. "Zane, I don't think I want to go anywhere."

His lips trailed along her shoulder, settled at the base

of her neck, lingered. He lifted his head and met her gaze in the mirror. "Anticipation makes the meal all the sweeter," he whispered, his eyes pools of heat and light. Holding her gaze in the glass, he trailed one elegant hand over the bare flesh above her bodice, then lower, over her breast. Claire watched his fingers, felt the tantalizing brush, and her knees were suddenly shaky. "First, we'll eat," he said. "Then we'll feast."

Mesmerized, she nodded, her imagination filled with images of him. "Feast," she echoed. "Oh, yes."

Zane had known that he was attracted to Claire Franklin—she'd been driving him crazy for days. But tonight, she took his breath away.

He had not wanted to leave the room, but his plan required their absence, and he had also wanted to show her that he could be civilized at times, that he knew how to wear a suit and order wine. He had arranged the evening to that end.

But as he stood in the hallway, staring at the beauty in the black dress, he felt a pain slice through his chest, and wondered if maybe this evening was a way for him to don his armor.

As they'd driven into Seattle this morning, as he waited for her answer to whether she would stay with him tonight, he'd been miserable. On the drive, he'd thought of little else but the impending loss of her.

Even worse had been the surge of relief and joy and…need that filled him when she'd said she would stay. Holding her in that moment had been a dizzying sensation, and it scared him. Scared him to think what it might mean.

And maybe the whole suit-and-tie, fancy-restaurant game was a way to put her at arm's length. Remind her—and himself—that he wasn't what he had seemed these past few days.

But somehow, none of that mattered when he looked into her eyes. He simply took her hand and told himself he owed her a nice evening, to make up for what she'd suffered by having the bad luck to rent him a room in her bed-and-breakfast. Bad luck for her. Quite another kind of fortune for him.

Seated at the table in a restaurant playing traditional Christmas carols, with candles burning and a scent of pine in the air, he forgot everything in Claire's delight. She had a critical eye for detail and quality in service, and the restaurant pleased her very much. Over a Christmas meal of baked Cornish hens and delicate dressing, she smiled. "Is this more instruction on how to manage Christmas for guests?"

"Not at all. It's for you. So you have a Christmas Eve dinner."

"Really?"

He lifted a shoulder, feeling an alien sense of shyness. "Yeah."

"What would you be celebrating if you were home?"

"Home in Paris?" he asked. "Or do you mean home at my mother's house?"

"Your mother's house. What did your family do on Christmas Eve?"

He took a sip of wine. A very small sip from the only glass he would allow himself. "Let's see...she would make supper. Something kind of different—she did fondues sometimes or some other kind of unusual thing. Usually, she let me open one present from the pile under the tree." He cut a tender bit of meat and let himself savor it before he went on. "Then we went to church."

"Oh, of course."

"Did you ever go?"

A flutter of lashes, the straightness of her spine. "No. Can't say that I ever have."

He inclined his head, thinking of her comment about the ocean and God. "You'd like Christmas Eve at church. Christmas carols and candles. It was the one time I didn't mind getting dragged over there."

"There was a little church not far from my house." She turned her fork, as if watching the light catch in the silver. "It was some kind of evangelical place, you know, like the Brothers and Sisters of the All-Loving Christ or something. Very small. But it was like a church in a painting. White clapboard and purple windows. They did a midnight service on Christmas Eve every year, and it always seemed magical."

"Why didn't you go?"

"Same reason I still don't. It seems like a place where you should know the rules."

For reasons he couldn't name, the confession saddened him. "I'll take you, if you like. Someone is bound to have a midnight service we can attend." He winked. "I promise I know the rules."

"Oh, no," she protested. "You don't have to do that."

"I don't have to do anything else, either." He lifted a finger to call the waiter over to the table. "Can you tell me if there is a church nearby that has a candlelight service at midnight?"

"Zane!"

He grinned at her and held up a hand. The waiter smiled. "Mass?"

"Not unless there is nothing else." He shot a glance at Claire. "Rules are different at mass."

"You're in luck, sir," the waiter said. "It just so happens that Ascension Episcopal is right up the street, and they have one of the most beautiful services in the city."

"Excellent. Thank you."

Claire looked at him with a pensive expression—and just that fast, he was slammed again by her physical beauty tonight. Candlelight caught in the honey-colored hair, swept up into a chignon with artless bits of hair trailing down her neck, around her face. Her eyes, wide and deep, were as still and beautiful as a lake at morning. "This church business isn't for me at all, is it?" she asked. "You want to go."

He glanced away, then back. Took a breath. "I always go on Christmas Eve. I'll go alone if you really hate the idea, but I'd much rather you went with me." He cleared his throat and admitted the truth. "Considering everything, I'd feel very superstitious about skipping tonight."

Flickers of something he couldn't quite catch made her eyes luminous. Lightly, she said, "You want to get on the Big Guy's good side, I guess, huh?"

Grateful that she didn't make it a big deal, he grinned. "Pretty much."

"Better safe than sorry." She touched his hand lightly. "I'd be glad to go along. Maybe I'll learn something."

"Maybe you will."

It was the most singularly painful evening of Claire's life. Zane held her hand as they strolled the quiet streets in a light snow, admiring window displays and the stillness of winter deepening the somehow sacred spirit of the evening. A spotlight scanned the clouds, and Claire wondered at the old tradition. Were they looking for Santa Claus or the Star of Bethlehem, or did anyone even remember?

They talked, easily and with much laughter, in the way of old friends or even siblings. Freely. Claire gave him stories she never told anyone, and he returned the favor, telling her about a childhood she discovered was almost as lonely as her own.

She loved everything about him. She liked his size and his hair, and that rueful twist of his mouth when he made some wry joke. She loved the starry beauty of his eyes and the rumbling sound of his voice, and his lean, long-fingered hand, holding hers.

And more. She liked his sense of humor and his ability to tease her, and his easy flirtatiousness and his good mind.

But all night, there was a piece of him missing. Aloof or hidden, she couldn't decide. He'd made no move toward her physically, and Claire was beginning to think she'd misread the situation. Were they going to be lovers? Or had he changed his mind?

It was as if they were going backward. They'd started out intimately connected on a mental plane, but as the moment of their physical intimacy neared, the emotional link was slipping.

And it made her feel like some kind of sex-crazed monster that she was so frustrated about it. All she could think about was his skin and her need to feel it against her. His mouth had mesmerized her over dinner. His voice poured like brandy down her spine. His fingers, moving softly between her own, were as erotic as a long, long kiss.

Truth be told, she didn't want to go to church. She wanted to go back to the hotel and make love. Twice, she opened her mouth to say that, and twice shut it again almost immediately.

So she had to bite down a sigh when they walked up from the rear of a brick church, filling with a stream of people. How boring could you get? Church. With a bad guy spy who was supposed to be so dangerous.

Oh, yeah, such a bad guy.

He stopped on the sidewalk before ascending the stairs, and grinned. "I sense a little discontent." His eyes danced. "Is there something else you'd rather be doing?"

She raised her eyebrows. "No, not a thing."

He lifted her hand to his mouth and kissed the palm. "Sure?"

"Of course."

She should have been warned by the glitter in his eyes, by the mischief on his mouth, but until he opened his mouth and swirled his tongue along her palm, she had no clue. "Liar," he said.

She snatched back her hand, and he captured her close, pulling her body up next to his in the wool suit, hips to hips, and Claire felt the thrust of his arousal. "That dress is driving me insane," he said.

"Is it?"

"You have the finest rear end in twelve countries." His hand slid down and covered that portion of her anatomy wickedly. "And I chose this dress just to show it off."

Relief washed through her, relief at the evidence of a desire that matched her own, and relief that she'd been wrong. "Zane, you could have given me a hint that you were still interested. I've been worrying all night that I was just a sex-crazed slut.''

He laughed. ''You could never be a slut,'' he said, ''but I love the sound of sex-crazed.'' Glancing over his shoulder, he pulled her into a deep shadow cast by the buttresses of the church and pushed her against the wall. ''Show me,'' he whispered. He kissed her hard, and devilishly slid a hand under her skirt, to caress her stocking-clad thigh. A low, hungry noise came out of his throat.

She nearly swooned at the shock of it. And the pleasure. And gladly she illustrated her need of him in return, letting her hands move on his thighs and the high round of his lean hips. She felt his hand move higher, cupping her bottom under her dress, and she kissed his throat, openmouthed.

He pressed into her, the whole length of him against the whole length of her. She arched into the rigid flesh that nudged urgently at her belly, and lifted her face for his kiss.

And oh, what a kiss! His sensual lips and thrusting, fencing tongue illustrated passion edged with restraint, need woven with honor, and the deeper he drew her, the closer they melded, the more intense the dichotomy became.

''Okay,'' he said, abruptly lifting his head. His breath came in a ragged tear from his throat and he leaned his forehead against hers. ''Enough for now.''

She had known he was a master of these things. She had not known, had not guessed, what intensity her own desire could take. She gripped his lapels and whispered, ''I am going to attack you when we get back to that room.''

He kissed her. ''Ditto.'' Then, straightening his suit,

smoothing her dress, he pulled her by her hand out of the shadows and up the steps, to take a candle from a boy dressed in a choir robe.

Zane did not let go of her hand, not then, and not when they sat down in a pew next to an elderly couple. Claire felt a strange sense of dizziness when she looked at him and saw a lock of his hair had come loose, drifting down over his high-boned cheek as he read the program. "Some of my favorite carols," he whispered, and bumped her shoulder playfully to point to them.

It was a boyish gesture and Claire smiled. He seemed to sense her staring, and raised his eyes. "What?"

Claire shook her head, overcome with such a sense of connection and love for him that she couldn't speak. She tucked the loose hair back into place, feeling proprietary and protective, like a wife.

And a sudden sense of despair struck her. All her life, she'd been so careful, following the rules and making sure she saved and used dental floss and didn't eat too many fats. She'd done everything by the book.

And how had fate rewarded her? Not with some really normal guy who grew giant pumpkins for a hobby and liked to putter around the house. Oh, no. She'd fallen—hard—for a burned-out espionage agent who had an appointment with death.

"You rat," she whispered.

As if he sensed her feelings, he tightened his grip on her hand. "Don't think about anything but now, Claire. This is what we have."

Throat tight, she nodded. At that moment, the lights in the church began to dim, and from the choir rose the first notes of "O Come, All Ye Faithful." Zane pulled her to her feet, scrambling for the hymnal so they could follow along with the words.

Claire had hummed under her breath nearly every waking moment of her life, and when she was in private, she sang aloud. But she knew she sang off-key, that she had no sense of carrying a tune. But next to her, Zane sang with all his heart, full-throated, full-chested, on tune and very nicely. She looked up at him, astonished again, and he winked. "Sing!" he whispered.

"I can't carry a tune."

"So? I sing loud enough to drown you out."

Hesitantly, she picked up the refrain, and it didn't sound too terrible with everyone else singing. To her surprise, she even started to enjoy it. As they sang one song, then another, the candles everyone held were lit, one to the other, to the other, until the big church was filled with the bright, warm light of the single flames held in the hands of all the worshippers. It was almost unbearably beautiful.

All of it was. The spirit of the night filled the beautiful old church, which smelled of dust and evergreen and perfume. She loved the celebratory hymns and the readings and the children sleepy on the shoulders of their parents. When a bell choir played an old hymn, Claire felt a swell of joy so intense she hardly knew how to express it. She leaned over and whispered, "Thank you for bringing me."

He squeezed her hand.

As they drifted out, the bells rang in celebration: *the Lord is come!* And Claire drifted beside Zane in a cloud of love and peace and gratitude.

Outside, he took her hand. "Thank you for going

with me.'' He waved at a cab. ''Now, let's get back to
the hotel.''

She raised her head, hearing the bells of Christmas
echo through her, and love as pure and clean as an
ocean morning filled her. ''Yes.''

Chapter 12

Zane unlocked the door of the hotel room, feeling a tingle of anticipation down the back of his neck. He pushed the door open, saw that things were in place and gestured for Claire to enter ahead of him.

Unsuspecting, she swirled in, shedding her wrap and kicking off her shoes nearly automatically. It took a long moment before she noticed, first, the flickering candles on the table. She straightened and, very slowly, turned in a circle. Then she stopped in the middle of the room, very still. Zane heard her exclaim, a quiet, broken little "Oh!"

"Merry Christmas," he said softly.

This was the one thing he could give her. Christmas. The hotel staff had done an excellent job. The room was alight with candles, burning on every surface—red and green ones, small and large, tapers and tabletops. He'd originally imagined the scene with all the same candles, burning at the same rate, but on Christmas

Eve, he'd had to make do with what he could find. To his pleasure, they looked even nicer like this, some flickering tall and some short.

The flames filled the room with a pale yellow glow that illuminated the small tree set up and decorated in the corner, a tree with presents of various sizes piled up beneath it. He'd run out of time in the end, but the pile still looked suitably large to him. On the wall, he'd hung a stocking with her name written on it in gold. He'd even managed to get bags of hard candies that the staff had put in crystal bowls, and candy canes to hang from the branches.

She still hadn't moved, and Zane wondered uneasily if maybe it had been too much. "Uh...I thought you should have a real Christmas," he said. "It was the one thing I could think of to pay you back."

She turned, and her face was shining, brilliant with light that burst from within her and glowed from her pores. And there were tears streaming down her face. "Zane," she said, and her voice broke. She simply moved across the room and flung herself into his arms, gripping him so tightly he could barely breathe.

And finally, finally, all the waiting was over. An explosion of something he was very afraid might be love rushed through him, lighting his nerves on fire as it went, like the single candles in the hands of the worshippers at church, one to the next to the next, until his entire body glowed. "I have protection now," he whispered.

And he kissed her.

And this time, he held nothing back. He let all the passion, all the need he'd been fighting swell up and spill over. Everything. He kissed her with all of his emotion on his mouth and in his heart. Her lips tasted of tears and goodness, a goodness he did not deserve but wanted to sup, anyway. It hurt to kiss her, hurt deep in his chest. It hurt to touch the elegant smoothness of her shoulders. It hurt that he could not seem to go slowly, as he had imagined, but wanted her, now, all of her, close to all of him.

He let her go, but whispered, when she would have released him, "Don't stop kissing me," and she gripped his face, standing on her toes, so that she didn't stop. So that her mouth was a nectar over his own, so that he drank of her flavor as he shucked his coat and unfastened his belt and kicked off his shoes. She took over, her hands on the buttons of his shirt as eager as his own on the zipper of her dress. He made a low noise as her hands lit on his bare chest, and he could not wait to hold her close for at least a moment. He touched her back, sliding his hands up the long, smooth expanse, dizzy with the wonder of her flesh.

She stepped back. "This isn't graceful," she said, and shimmied out of her stockings, leaving them in a filmy pile on the floor. Raising smoky eyes, she said, "Take off your clothes, Zane," and lifted her hands to her hair, pulling out the pins.

He didn't move as she shook her head, sending the hair scattering over her arms, then carefully took the shoulders of her dress from her arms and pulled it off over her head. His heart thudded in perfect anticipation as he watched her body revealed an inch at a time. Her knees and then her thighs and the teal velvet panties and her belly, faintly curved, and her breasts in the velvet bra.

There was nothing shy about her as she met his gaze, smiling in that timeless, womanly way, knowing the effect she had. And he gave, gladly, what she wanted, his purest, most passionate gaze, admiring her shoulders, shining white and delicate in the candlelight, and the rise of her breasts in the dark velvet, and her smooth belly and white legs.

In sudden impulse, he moved, and in the candlelit room, he put his hands on her shoulders and turned her to face the mirror. "Look at you," he said, meeting her gaze as he had earlier. "Look at us."

He moved his hands, watching his fingers slide over her flesh. He watched as he pushed the straps from her shoulders, and drew the velvet slowly from her breasts. A low, deep pounding of anticipation filled his blood as he peeled the fabric away, and her breasts, pert and round and white, were revealed. He reached behind her and unfastened the garment, and it fell to the floor, leaving her naked except for her panties. He stepped close, pressing his hips into her buttocks, and then spread his hands over her belly. His fingers were dark against her skin, and his breath left him as he watched those hands he'd known all of his life slide upward to cup her breasts, flesh he'd never known but which felt familiar to him. The supple weight settled into each palm, and she made a sound as she covered his hands with her own, watching in the mirror.

With a pounding heat in his loins, he reveled in the duality of feeling the exquisite softness of her flesh and seeing the beauty of the rose-and-white breasts in his big dark hands in the mirror. He thought he would never forget the sight as long as he lived. "How beautiful," he said.

"Yes," she whispered. She turned in his embrace. "Now you."

Her naked breasts brushed his rib cage and he sucked

in a breath, closing his eyes as she unfastened his pants and pushed them down his legs, leaving him naked.

"You lied," she said. "You don't have cupid boxer shorts."

"I left them off," he whispered, putting his hands on her shoulders and stepping close.

She stopped him. "I want to look at you," she said shyly.

Not even the candlelight would hide everything, and he held her for a moment, groaning as she lightly touched the engorged weight between his legs. "I am not…"

She stepped around behind him. "Beautiful?" she asked. She pressed her body into his back, and he groaned at the press of her breasts, the alluring whisper of a thigh along his leg. He closed his eyes, knowing that a naked woman was a beautiful thing, but a naked, aroused male was only ridiculous.

"Open your eyes, Zane," she said quietly. "Watch as I touch you, too." She put her hands on his belly and spread them open, and to please her, he did as she asked.

One leg was thinner than the other, and whiter, and weak, and the ropy scars marred his knee. Her small, slim hand touched that leg, and the ruddy scar, and moved again, touching all of them, the marks of shrapnel and the old bullet wound on his side and the scar he got jumping out of a tree when he was eight.

She stood behind him and ducked her head around his arm. "You are beautiful, too, Zane." She stroked his belly, touched his organ lightly. "So beautiful."

He turned and took her into his embrace, poised for one long moment to simply absorb the feeling of her skin pressed against his own, her softness and small-

ness sending an ache through him that was equal parts
joy and need. She kissed him this time. Kissed the ruined places on his body, the marks and scars of his life.
She kissed his arm. His leg. The white puckered mark
on his hipbone, the long scar across his chest.

It was a million times more than he deserved, but he
accepted it, touching her golden head, her white shoulders, her slim arms, until he could bear no more. He
hauled her up and kissed her, long and deep, feeling
the breath fly from them as their bodies swayed, slid,
brushed.

"I am still no beauty, as you are," he whispered,
and knelt, sliding his hands all the way down her body,
to finally kiss her breasts. He mustered control enough
to kiss the pert rose tips lightly, then flicker his tongue
over them, each in turn. She trembled faintly.

He paused. "Claire, I need to know—are you a virgin?"

Her hands moved to his hair, and there was a tug,
and she put her hands in the looseness, lifting it and
letting it fall over her hands with a quiet sigh. "No."
She smiled faintly. "Sorry."

"Good." He opened his mouth and took her breast
between his lips, suckling fiercely, till she forgot touching his hair and her hands were curled like claws on
his shoulders, and then, only then, did he slide his
hands between her legs, to the heat waiting there for
his questing fingers, and touch her.

Please her. She writhed a little against him—"Zane,
I need to touch you!"

"Wait," he whispered, a promise of pleasure. Moving again to the pert, eager tip of her breast, he suckled
her, drawing forth a new cry as he peeled away her

panties, stoked the fires higher and higher, feeling the looseness in her limbs, the tautness in her hands.

With one clean move, he knelt and drew her down and pulled her, hard, to him, a deep, full thrust that made them cry out together, and grip each other, and fight for control.

''Don't move,'' he said, but she wrapped her arms around his neck and brushed her breasts against his chest and then kissed him, her nimble tongue flickering over his lips until he could pause no more. He opened his mouth and kissed her and she groaned, and he felt the pulse of her response in a hard squeeze around him.

''Hold on,'' he whispered. ''Don't move, Claire.''

He brushed her breast and bent his head to her neck, and then there was no turning back. His own need overwhelmed him and he bit her shoulder with a wild kind of violence, like a stallion with a mare, letting the fury rage until they were bucking, moving in almost frenzied fury together, and she bit him back, bit his neck, grazed his shoulder. They moved in a deep rocking movement, and he thought, as she burst around him, that he'd never understood this till now. Never understood the binding it made.

And then he was lost in his own release, following her into a gilded swell of sensation that caught them, mingled their souls, and sent them, as bits of shattered light, back to themselves.

Claire gripped him close, her arms tight around his shoulders, her knees skinned from the rug and the wild abandon of the moment. Her heart pounded and she could feel sweat where their flesh met. His face was buried in her shoulder, and she could feel the sting of a mark he'd made on her, and his arms were as tight around her as hers were around him. They breathed hard together, and dizziness made her feel light-headed.

He lifted his head first, and Claire shifted to look at him. Nothing could have prepared her, not even the shattering moments that had just passed, for what she saw in his sober eyes. For a long moment, he simply looked at her, touching her face gently, touching the bones as if to memorize them. It made her ache because she understood and didn't want to, that he would leave.

So she put her hands on his face, too, and they touched each other, still joined, touched noses and lips, and finally, moved close to kiss very sweetly, hands cupped around each other's face. "Let's move to the bed," he whispered.

He stood for a moment in the candlelight, looking down at her, before he climbed in next to her and pulled the covers over them. They lay, face-to-face, arms entangled, and kissed.

And kissed. And kissed. Below the covers, hands moved, learning the contours of precious flesh. He skimmed his hands down her back, over her buttocks, down her thighs, around to her breasts and belly and arms. She stroked his chest and back, his shoulders and hands, the always surprisingly velvet flesh of his organ.

Only then did he lift up on one elbow and bend his head over her breasts, his hair falling in black splendor upon her flesh. She watched, oddly breathless as he bent and took her breast into his mouth. His eyes closed as if in bliss, and Claire knew she would never forget the sight. Never. She shifted, and he came to her, slowly this time, looking at her eyes as they joined, slowly, slowly, slowly, an inch at a time. And when the joining was complete, he lowered his face and kissed her. "I want to stay right here. Always."

She closed her eyes, maybe against the intimacy of his dark green eyes looking into her own while there was such a deep connection, and arched into him. "Okay," she whispered.

A dozen times, a hundred, she'd thought of what it would be like to be with him this way. But she'd underestimated everything. She underestimated the power of her physical response, her ability to embrace the erotic, her ability to feel pleasure, her explosive response to it.

She thought she'd known how much she wanted this particular man, too, but she'd underestimated that as well. The sound of his sighs, the tickle of laughter she managed to tease from him, the roaring heat of his need of her made her burn.

She thought she'd understood what the term "making love" meant.

And she'd not even had a clue. As they wound through the night, coming together over and over, she learned to give and receive pleasure in ways she'd never dreamed she could, and found she only wanted to know more, and the more she gave, the more she had. Each kiss, each brush, each time they fell, breathing each other's breath, in exhaustion, she felt her soul more entwined with his. She ached with it. Ached with loving him and having to keep those words inside her.

When they slept, sated, they slept entwined, shifting together, breathing together, as if they were no longer two apart, but joined as one being.

A knock awakened them, and Claire stirred sleepily, feeling Zane jump up. "Cover up," he said with a chuckle.

"Who is it?"

"Room service," he said, leaping out of bed. He stood in the cloudy early morning light completely naked, looking for something to cover himself with, and Claire giggled. He looked gorgeous, his hair tousled and streaming down over the broad, powerful shoulders, his long back sinewy and strong as he grabbed his discarded trousers. The knock sounded again. "I'm coming," he said, scrambling into the pants and tossing his hair out of his face. At the door, he paused and waved at her. Claire laughed and ducked under the covers.

She listened to the sound of the tray being rolled in, and the two men made small talk, then she heard the door shut. She poked her head out, and Zane was diving for her, like a lion cub leaping on a new toy. She shrieked good-naturedly and ducked away. He grabbed her, covers and all, and growled, kissing the top of her head. "Come on, get up, get up! Gotta see what Santa left you."

Tugging the covers from her head, she looked around. "Santa?"

His grin was infectious. "Yeah." He hopped up, only limping a little, and went to the tree. He looked at the labels. "To Claire," he read aloud, and tossed it to her. "To Claire." A toss. "Yep, Claire again."

The boxes thudded into her lap, and Claire laughed, catching them. "Zane! I need coffee."

"Nope." He threw her a candy cane from the tree. "Candy first. It's a rule." He took one for himself and tore the wrapping off and stuck it in his mouth, then dipped down to pull one more gift from beneath the tree, and tossed it over.

Claire, holding the covers to her breasts and the

candy cane in her hand, saw suddenly what he must have been like as a boy. The candy cane stuck out of his mouth like a cigar, making a bulge in his elegant cheek, and with only his pants on and his hair falling round his face, it was easy to see him in railroad train pajama bottoms and scruffy house shoes, dancing around a tree on Christmas morning.

It was also easy to imagine what he would be like as a father. And a swell of something lost welled up in her. For one long moment, she let herself see him, in the big warm living room at the inn, a small boy and girl at his feet, as he unleashed all that happy energy.

"Come on!" he said around the candy cane. "You have to tear 'em open. No prissy unpinning-the-edges kind of junk."

"One tiny sip of coffee?"

He grinned. "Nope." He sat on the edge of the bed and unwrapped the candy cane. "Try it."

Laughing, she stuck it in her mouth. He promptly took it out again and kissed her. "Mmm...you sure are sweet tasting," he said, waggling his eyebrows.

She stuck the cane in her mouth again. "I think if I don't get grown-up coffee before candy, then kisses should definitely be off-limits."

"Have it your way." He plucked a box from her lap. "Here, open this one."

Suddenly shy, she turned it over, looking for the flap to loosen it.

"Rip it, Claire." He reached over and yanked the paper hard, tearing a big gash into it. "Rip into it like you ripped into me. Think greed."

She laughed at that, then squeezed her eyes shut and

tore it wildly, as fast as she could. When she saw what it was, she blinked. "Barbie soaps?"

He sucked on the candy cane, mischief in his eyes. "Maybe those could go in your own personal bathroom. Now, you say 'cool' and toss it over your shoulder and do this one."

She laughed, and was much relieved to discover she wasn't going to be opening a bunch of embarrassingly expensive trinkets. She tossed the box over her shoulder and tore into the others, finding Barbie towels and a plastic brush-and-comb set with Barbie on the spines. The last one was the biggest, and by then, she had the game down pat. She ripped open the package, expecting maybe a board game or a Barbie mouse pad.

Instead, there was a beautifully dressed doll in a gold dress, with gilt in her floor-length braid.

"Rapunzel," she whispered. A thousand thoughts rushed through her mind as she stared at that beautiful, beautiful doll—a dozen little-girl memories of standing in a toy store with her eyes on some doll in velvet and gilt, waiting for some lucky girl to open her on Christmas morning. It pierced her deeply to understand that he'd somehow known that. Her vision blurred dangerously, but she looked at him and clasped the doll to her chest. "Cool," she whispered.

He brushed a tear away with his thumb and smiled around the candy cane. "That *is* the right reaction."

She raised her chin. "Zane Hunter, whatever you take with you out of this time with me, you take this. You're a good man with a good heart. No one, nothing, can ever destroy that."

His lashes hid his expression for a minute. "You make me better than I really am."

Remembering her own shopping yesterday, she

started to leap up, remembered she was naked below the covers, and hesitated. "Hand me your shirt," she said, "I have a surprise for you, too."

"Cool," he said, and dipped over to pick the shirt up off the floor. "We made a mess in here last night."

She slid her arms into the shirt, carefully closing it over herself before she let the covers fall, then tossed everything aside and padded across the room to dip into the drawer where she'd hidden his stocking. She brought it over and dropped it in his lap and settled beside him. "Santa left this for you."

He grinned, obviously pleased, and poured out the contents on the bed. "Hmm, an apple," he said, and with a cavalier toss, threw it over his shoulder. "Oooh, jelly beans. Better." His eyebrows lifted and he plucked out the bag of chocolate coins. "Pirate treasure. *Way* cool." He tore open the nylon and took out a coin, offering her one. When she shook her head, he rolled his eyes. "Gotta work on that greed thing, Claire, I'm telling you." He unwrapped a coin—a small one, she noticed—and popped it into his mouth. "Ahoy, matey! What's this?" He picked up the white box in the midst of everything else, and flipped the lid off with his thumb.

For a moment, she really couldn't tell what he thought of the green turtle. "It matches your eyes," she said.

Those glorious eyes lifted, and she saw a shine in them. "And now I'll have a turtle story."

She laughed. "Yes! I was afraid you wouldn't remember that you told me turtle stories that day on the ferry."

"I get it." He pushed it aside, along with soaps and towels and candy and torn wrappings, and tumbled her to the bed. "What else do I get, hmm?" He pinned her arms and unbuttoned the first of the buttons on the shirt. "What's wrapped up in here?"

Claire gazed at him sleepily. "I don't know. Open it up and find out."

"Yeah? Maybe I need to feel it a little first, see if I can guess." His hand rubbed up her ribs, covered a breast. "Hmm. Nice and plump. Let me see."

He unbuttoned the next two buttons, as if he was rushing to tear open a package, and shoved the cloth away, then made a low, approving noise. "Mmm. Just what I wanted." His nostrils flared, and against her hip, she felt his interest, which intensified as he simply looked at her breasts. Her heart shivered a little as he moved his fingers and touched one nipple. A half grin crossed his mouth. "Look at that! It grows."

She laughed and pushed him over on his back. "That's not the only thing that grows, is it?" she said archly, straddling him. "I bet I can make it grow even more."

He grinned up at her and lifted his hands, sliding them inside the shirt. "But you aren't anywhere near as greedy as I am," he said.

"You ain't seen nothin' yet, sugar," she said.

Chapter 13

Zane lingered with her over croissants and sliced smoked salmon and strawberries. They pulled the cart over to the bed and sprawled over the covers, half-dressed, eating and drinking and talking lazily.

It was the most peaceful time he could remember. Impulsively, he bent over and kissed her. "Thank you, Claire."

She lifted a wicked brow, sucking on a strawberry. "The pleasure is mine, sir, I assure you." She must have seen something in his face, because her expression sobered suddenly. "Oh, don't say it's time. Not yet."

He smoothed a hand over her hair. "Not quite. But we have to check out by noon, and then…"

"Don't say it." She pressed her mouth together. "We both know what comes next." She tossed the strawberry top aside and took his hand. "I need a shower. Let me wash your hair."

"My hair?"

She put a hand in it, drew it around her wrist. "Yes."

Such a small thing, a small act and a small request. Zane couldn't figure out why it made him feel such a stab of pain. He nodded and let himself be tugged to his feet.

The pain stayed with him the whole time she was busy with pulling the shower curtain and turning on the water. Standing at the door, listening with half his mind while she hummed "We Three Kings" under her breath, he remembered the first motel room they had stayed in, when Coach had whined at the door and he'd heard her weeping in the shower. He remembered how much he'd wanted her then, and it seemed like a very long time ago, seemed like he'd known her for years and years. The way she bent her head now, tugging his oversize shirt close to her body while she stuck the other arm in the water to test the temperature, was intimately familiar, and he knew suddenly that he would see it again and again in the coming months, that it would flash into his mind without warning. He would miss the breathy softness of the broken tune that ran underneath every moment of her day and the way she rubbed her dog's ears in moments of stress, a heartbreaking legacy from her childhood. He would miss—

Everything.

He braced his hands on the doorway, overcome.

She turned and unbuttoned his shirt, shedding it without a hint of self-consciousness, and he ached with something like gratitude. "It's ready," she said with a warm smile, holding out a hand. "Come on." A twinkle lit her eyes. "Unless you're shy."

He shook his head and shed his trousers and joined her, but the ache did not leave him. It grew, edging into his spirit like some creeping monster from the black lagoon, while she made him sit and then wet his hair, and washed it, an act she performed with odd sobriety, her hands lingering along the edges of his scalp, on his shoulders as she spread the wet strands over his back, then rinsed the soap, making him close his eyes. And while his eyes were still closed, she bent into the spray and kissed his wet mouth with her own, making water pool and drip between their faces, and he couldn't help the swell of need that rose in him, not a need to make love again, but a need to hold on to her, keep kissing her, for a long, long time, prolonging the moment when the water would be shut off and they had to dry off and put on their clothes, and—

So he pulled her into his lap and forced himself to laugh and play and swirl soap over her pretty breasts as if he were lustful instead of just needy. And there was a catch in his throat when she turned to him, as if she knew what was behind his game, and circled his neck with her arms and just held him very tightly. They didn't speak, didn't move, just embraced for a time he wished was endless, but was not. The seconds ticked away as the rush of water drowned out all sounds, and then the minutes, and then, shivering, wrinkled, they had to get out.

In silence, then, they dressed. Zane tried not to look at anything. The bed was rumpled with their lovemaking, and littered with bits of paper from the morning's spree. Their discarded clothing was on the floor and had to be gathered, shaken, packed away. Claire carefully tucked her gifts into an oversize department store bag, and he tried not to notice that she broke a branch

off the Christmas tree and tucked it inside with everything else. Finding he had a sentimental streak as well,
he folded the stocking she'd given him and put it in
his pack. The turtle he put into his pocket—a good luck
charm, maybe.

Finally, there was nothing else to do, and as if he
understood he was finally going to get out of his prison,
Coach happily padded over to the door and whined.

Zane checked his gun and holstered it under his arm.
''Ready?''

She took a breath and looked around. Nodded.

In the lobby, they approached the desk to check out,
and the pleasant young clerk typed the room number
into the computer. ''Did you enjoy your stay?''

Zane was not in the mood for small talk. ''Yes.''

''It looks like a fax came in for you, Mr. Knightley.
Hold on and let me get it for you.''

''Mr. Knightley?'' Claire said beside him, chuckling.

A prickle lifted the hairs of his neck, and Zane
frowned, nerves suddenly taut. Casually, he looked
over his shoulder. Two waitresses from the lobby restaurant stood at the door, the rooms behind them obviously empty. A man in a gray flannel suit read the
paper, a briefcase at his feet. There was no one else in
sight.

''Here you are,'' the clerk said. ''Came in late last
night, but there was a Do Not Disturb order on your
door.''

Forcing himself to take it without revealing his urgency, Zane scanned it quickly. It was from Max, the
point of origin and name scrambled, and only had a
single address, which meant the safe house location had
changed. His nerves rippled. Why?

But conscious of both Claire and the clerk watching

him, he simply nodded. "Thank you." Hiking the pack on his shoulder, he took Claire's elbow and unobtrusively tucked the paper into her pocket. As they walked toward the entrance, he said quietly in her ear, "If anything goes wrong, get to this address as quickly as possible. They'll take care of you."

"Has something gone wrong?"

Now not only were his nerves taut, but there was a warning roar in his ears. "I'm not sure," he said, wanting to hurry her along. But obviously something had happened; if they were changing safe houses this late in the game, it was likely a security breach.

He glanced over her shoulder as the elevator doors opened. There was only a slight edge of relief when he saw a young woman and a baby in a stroller come out of the doors. "Let's just get out of here."

There was a revolving door at the entrance, and Zane let Claire take the first rotation, and he glanced over his shoulder as he stepped in. The woman with the stroller had stopped to speak to the clerk. In an instant, he cataloged details—small and slim, dark-haired. He focused on the stroller, but the baby was bundled in pale green blankets, and he couldn't see it.

Urgently, he stepped behind Claire and rushed her along the street and ducked into a doorway about a half a block down. Quickly, he readied his gun, taking grim comfort in the cold, solid weight of it.

"Don't move," he said, putting a hand on her shoulder and keeping her in place while he ducked around the doorway to watch the hotel entrance. The woman had been dressed for a cold day, and the baby, bundled in blankets, had been ready for the weather, too. Surely the woman was coming out.

The street was deserted, and he remembered with a shock that it was Christmas Day.

A dark car pulled up in front of the hotel, and a uniformed driver came around to open the door for the man in the gray flannel suit. With him was the woman, who now carried the child, crying in protest, his face red and his fists flailing.

Zane let out a breath. Narrowing his eyes, he looked in both directions, his nerves still alert. Something was wrong.

Abruptly, he said, "Change of plan, darlin'. I have to make a phone call."

Claire knew there was a problem the minute the clerk handed over the fax. But then, she'd known everything had changed before they'd even left their room. There she'd watched her lover, that boyishly exuberant Santa Claus, the one who sang in church and found beautiful dolls for the neglected child she'd been, disappear as he dressed. The shell was built one degree at a time, as he slipped into jeans and boots and a simple chambray shirt. He combed his hair and pulled it back, and stuck on his hat, and the Zane she knew was swallowed by Hunter. By the time he asked her if she was ready to go, his eyes were no longer twinkling and soft. Even in the frame of spiky, long lashes, they were unmistakably hard.

It had shaken her a little to see him check his gun. He planned to kill someone today.

Or be killed.

But then, for an instant, she'd had the old Zane, when she heard the name he'd used to register. Mr. Knightley? She wanted to tease him about Jane Austen, but the swift, almost imperceptible ripple of alarm on his face when the clerk said he had a fax had stopped her.

And as if his body was now an extension of her own, she could feel the tension radiating from him, tension and—worry.

Hurrying along beside him now, it dismayed her. She had seen him angry. She'd seen him protective. She'd seen him cool and calm under fire. She had not felt, not even when she said she'd used a credit card, a sense of worry before.

It frightened her. Not because she feared that fate could replace cold, calculating reason with worry, but because she suspected she was the reason for it. If it were only Zane, he'd handle the situation, even coolly accepting his own death. He would not be so accepting of injury to Claire.

"Zane, can't you tell me what's going on?"

He was limping, not as if he were in pain, but in the manner of a man who has long borne the weakness of a limb and has learned to simply drag it along as best he can. The worry had frightened her; that determined but betraying weakness terrified her. He halted and turned to hail a cab, which, glad of the fare on this slow morning, pulled over immediately. "I'll explain later," he said gruffly, and shuffled her into the cab.

For a moment, she was afraid he was going to just dump her there, and she turned, reaching for his arm. When he tossed his pack to the floor, she curled her hand quickly into itself and bit back the plea in her mouth. He slammed the door.

"Where to?"

"I don't know," he said, glancing uneasily behind them. It was only his eyes that made the measuring dart, but Claire caught it. "We're tourists. Is there a park overlooking the Sound where we can have a winter picnic?''

"Sure thing." He pulled into traffic.

Zane made no move to comfort her. He settled stiffly on his side of the seat and stared out the window. His hands were curled into fists on his thighs, his face as stony as Mount Rushmore.

Get used to it, she told herself. He'd bid her farewell in the shower. To hide her sorrow, she stared out her own window, trying not to think about what was ahead—for either one of them.

At the park, the cab driver let them out, and Zane paid the driver, then looked around in a circle. Fog was rising from the ground, making him look as if he were floating, and Claire almost smiled over that, but his hard expression stopped her. "Come on," he said gruffly. "I have to find a phone."

A block or so away, they stopped at a phone on the corner. Claire, accustomed to giving him privacy on the phone, started to wander off, but he snagged her arm. "Stay right here."

A joke about spy talk rose to her lips, but she closed her lips before it spilled out. Zane punched in a long series of numbers and waited, his eyes moving, alert. Finally someone answered on the other end. "Max," Zane said. "What's up?"

Claire watched his jaw tighten as he heard the news. Bad news, obviously. She found herself reaching down to rub Coach's ears.

"I'll be there in a half hour," Zane said to the person at the other end of the line, and hung up. He looked at Claire. "Listen closely. There was a security breach— an insider has obviously been feeding information to the Ghost, and the safe house was hit last night. Three agents were killed, but she got away.''

Claire simply waited.

''I'm going to take you to my buddy Max, who will do whatever is necessary to make sure you're safe.''

Until now, she'd been reasonable and calm and accepting of whatever he said, but as he stood before her, weary and grim, she reached for his arms and gripped them beneath his coat. ''Zane, you don't have to do this. Let someone else bring her in.''

His green eyes were cold as emeralds. ''I can't.''

She bowed her head. ''Fine. Let's get this over with, then.''

They hailed a second cab and climbed in without saying a word.

Simone Chevalier dressed carefully. Black jeans with pencil-slim legs, the sensible black boots that she favored because they allowed much greater freedom of movement than heels of any kind. An ivory silk blouse, open to the third button to show an alluring rise of cleavage. A black woolen blazer over that. A jaunty black wool tam on her hair. Her revolver in the back of her jeans.

A touch of red lipstick and she was ready. Last night, the fool from the Organization had utterly destroyed her careful trap at the safe house, rushing in before the quarry was in place and drawing a good deal of unwelcome attention. When he arrived at her door, sheepish but hoping to be rewarded for good intentions, she had allowed him to think she was placated, then took him for a walk, promising sexual favors, and shot him on a bridge, watching coldly as his body fell to the dark water below. His absence would be noticed in a day or two; perhaps his body would be found sooner.

No matter. Today she had to strike, and she knew just how to do it. Picking up a slip of paper with the Seattle address of Max Azul, an address she'd coaxed from her clumsy lover, she smiled.

It was so convenient that Hunter had fallen in love. Men were so much easier to manage when they thought with something other than their brains. Simone was so grateful to Claire Franklin that she might even kill her first, to spare her the distress of her man's death.

Zane used the cab ride to clear his head. He closed his eyes and breathed deeply, focusing on that emotionless center of him that could track with cool efficiency. Everything else dropped away—Claire and love and dreams of a better future. There was only now. There were only his hands and his eyes and his cleverness to outwit his enemy.

By the time they reached the apartment near downtown, only a mile or two from the hotel where they'd slept, he was ready. Ready enough to notice the shades drawn at Max's window.

Zane swore. The shades were a warning.

Claire got out of the cab silently, and in the quiet day, he heard Coach's tags jingle. He paid the cab driver and took Claire's arm. "Walk with me for a minute and listen carefully." His grip on her arm was too tight, and he forced himself to ease off a bit.

There were more people out here—mostly young, probably single professionals unable to get away for the holidays. They gathered in little knots at a coffee stand on the corner and in front of a bakery whose owner obviously recognized the makeup of his neighborhood, and walked singly or jogged in pairs. A fairly steady flow of traffic moved on the street. Gritting his teeth, Zane ducked with Claire into an alley.

"Memorize this phone number," he said, and gave her the number to a high level official at the Organization. "Repeat it."

Claire, her eyes wide and frightened but not hysterical, did as asked.

Zane gave her instructions, a code word to use. "Then I want you to get to a restaurant and tell them to come and take you there."

"What if they don't believe me?"

He took a breath. "They will. Max has already been in touch. They'll be waiting for your call—actually mine, but they'll take care of you." He forced himself to step back. "All right. Go."

That chin came up. "Hold on. How do you even know all this? Psychic connections? Are you reading messages in the sky?"

"No." He pushed her shoulder a little. "There's no time to explain, Claire. You have to trust me one more time, and then it's over, I promise."

She stood on her toes and pressed a fierce kiss to his lips. "Be careful, Zane," she whispered, and turned to go.

Feeling a brittleness shatter in him, Zane grabbed her arm and kissed her fiercely. "Goodbye, Claire."

For one long moment, she stared at him intently, then she whirled and left him. He let go, then stepped out of the alley to watch her progress, tension in his gut. Letting her get a dozen paces ahead, he began to follow, scanning the on-coming foot traffic with the intentness of a lifetime of training.

She reached a phone on the corner. He paused, wishing he had a pack of cigarettes so he could feign stopping to light one. Where the hell was Max? He glanced at the shuttered windows, but nothing had changed. Still, Max was here. He would have seen Claire with him, and would move to protect her.

To stall, he slid his pack off his shoulder and set it on the sidewalk, opening one of the zippers as if looking for something. Surreptitiously, he scanned the area immediately surrounding Claire, looking for Max—and for any sign of a woman that might fit the profile of Simone Chevalier. There had been no photograph in her dossier, but the description had been very close to what Claire imagined—a pretty, small, elegant woman. Dark-haired.

A tall, slim man in a camel hair coat stepped out of a cigar shop near the phone. Urbane, every inch a Continental, the man paused to unwrap a cigar, as if relishing the pleasure on this cold, Christmas morning.

Max.

Relieved, Zane zipped the pocket and started to stand. At the halfway point between them, there was a loud crash, and startled, Zane leapt to his feet, poised for anything.

Three things happened simultaneously. He saw the accident on the street—a rear-end collision between a Subaru and a Lincoln. His knee screamed in protest. And the hairs on the back of his neck prickled.

Horns blared. Shouts and exclamations rose, and people ran to see if they could be of any assistance. Urgently Zane looked back to Claire, who was still on the telephone, one hand covering her free ear as she struggled to hear over the sudden cacophony. Max had moved a step or two closer—

And moving toward the telephone, coming up on

Claire's back, was a woman dressed in black. Black jeans. Black coat. Black hat. With a sudden shock, Zane recognized her from a bar in Rio.

He bolted, pulling his gun as he ran in focused pursuit, his body and mind a single, fierce force. He had no hope she'd hear him, but he cried out her name anyway—a warning, a hope. "Claire!"

Claire heard her name and whirled, dropping the phone. The street was filling up with traffic and confusion over the accident, and people stopped in front of her to observe from a safe distance. The cry came again. "Claire!"

At the moment she spied him, running at an impossible speed through the crowd, heedless of passersby he jolted or the dog he leapt over, an arm fell around her from behind. Claire screamed, dropping Coach's leash as she fought to free herself. A hand covered her mouth, hard, dragging her head back, and a voice said, "Max here. You're safe," before Coach leapt in protective, growling fury on the man. He yelped and released her.

Claire scrambled away and looked back to see Zane only a hundred paces away, still running with all his life. "Get down!" he cried.

Too late, Claire saw the small dark woman between them. Claire dipped to retrieve the leash and haul Coach away from Max, and the action saved her. A whoosh of soundless air zapped by her cheek and slammed with a ping into the phone behind. She reacted instinctively, falling flat on her belly, hauling her dog close.

But the Ghost had turned, straight and calm, and lifted her arm—

And fired.

Zane fell.

"No!" Claire moaned.

The whole scene took on a surreal quality. Claire felt as if everything were moving in slow motion. She saw the Ghost turn, slim and satisfied, and felt, at the same moment, Coach tear away from her grip. A movement nearby, which had to be Max. Zane moved, rolling to his feet with impossible grace after the hit he'd taken, and there was blood everywhere, dripping from Max's arm, spread over Zane's shoulder and forehead as he lifted that huge, black, menacing gun.

Even as she watched, Claire knew the scene was carved indelibly in her memory, saved in brilliant fragments: The overcast sky and cheerful fake velvet ribbons tied to lampposts. The slim young woman lifting her gun as Zane lifted his, like two gunslingers meeting at last in the streets of Laredo. Max, struggling to aim a gun with his left hand because his right had been bitten. The impossibility of no one noticing three big guns out on a street on a cold morning, because of a traffic accident.

And then there was Coach, a flying, deadly mass of gold and brown hurtling toward the threat, his fierce growl as he sprang—

Two shots rang out as the dog found his mark. Claire screamed, unable to choke it back, fearing for her lover and her dog and sure she was going to lose both.

The woman fell sideways under the weight of dog, and Claire saw with horror that another fount had opened on Zane's body. He swayed dangerously.

And like her dog, Claire sprang into action. The woman was not dead, and she slammed the butt of her gun into the dog's muzzle. With a fierce cry, Claire

raced toward her, seeing with a sense of sick triumph
that there was blood here, too, blood on the slim arm
and blood on her stomach. Claire kicked her, kicked
the arm, and the gun went flying.

Sirens cut through the confusion. Claire sprang toward the gun as the Ghost scrambled to her feet, vault-
ing for the same prize.

Claire got there first, and without a moment's
thought, she simply fell over it, feeling the metal slam
into her ribs.

Then there were police everywhere and flashing
lights. Claire, stunned, sat up, holding the gun close to
her so it could not be used as a weapon. She saw Zane
slumped against a trash can, and Coach crawled to him,
whimpering. The Ghost sprawled in a patch of grass,
and judging by the blood in a pool beside her, Claire
thought she was dead.

Shaking, Claire stood up. Holding the gun, she
walked dizzily toward Zane. Max knelt next to him, a
worried expression on his face, one he tried to erase as
Claire sank down, winded, beside them.

"How bad?"

But he didn't even have to answer. Claire saw the
wounds and stood up, screaming for an ambulance.

Coach whined, and Claire sank down in a daze and
buried her face in her dog's fur, probing him for signs
of injuries. A small cut marked his head, and there was
a goose egg beneath it, but he looked okay otherwise.

"Drop the gun and put your hands up!"

Claire looked up, dazed, to see who they were ar-
resting. Three policeman in uniform held their guns on
her. "Wait!" she said, "you don't understand! I was
just—"

Max leaned over and gently removed the gun from

her hand. "Just go along, Claire," he said, in an unusual accent. "I will take care of it, hmm?"

Finally, reality sank in. Clamping her mouth shut,
she opened her hands and stood up. "I wasn't doing
anything," she said. "Th-that woman back there…she
shot—" she glanced at Zane, overcome "—she hit my
dog…I mean…" A young police officer rushed toward
her, grabbing her arm with what she thought was un-
necessary force. "Hey! Aren't you listening? I didn't
do anything."

He clamped a handcuff around her wrist and then
slammed the other link around her other hand behind
her. "I can't go. He's hurt! And there's no one to take
my dog." When he tugged her elbow, she yanked
away. "Wait!"

Zane looked bad. His skin was unearthly pale, and
she could tell by the way he carefully did not move
that he knew it was bad, too. She fell to her knees,
welcoming the slam of pain as they struck the pavement, and bent forward to put her head against his
neck. "Don't you dare die," she whispered.

Then the policeman hauled her up and moved her
away, and she looked back to Max. "Take care of them
first!" she cried. "I'll be okay. Find out—" Then she
was cut off as an officer put a hand on her head and
unceremoniously sat her on the seat.

As they drove away, she saw an ambulance pull up
and two men burst out of the doors, heading for Zane.
"God, don't let him die," she prayed. "Please."

Chapter 14

If Claire had ever spent a more miserable two hours in her life, she couldn't remember them. The holding cell was cold and empty, and smelled faintly of mildew and illness and faint sweat. She didn't want to sit down, but eventually, her nerves gave out and she sank gingerly down at the edge of a bench screwed to the wall. Through the barred opening of the door, she could hear the workaday voices of employees at the desk, trading Christmas stories and children's escapades. The normality of the conversation only served to underscore the strangeness of the past few days. It depressed her.

As if to underscore the misery, somewhere beyond the jail, church bells began to ring, exuberant, cheerful, celebratory.

Pacing in the cold, echoey room, her thoughts skittered and jumped from one image to another—Zane and the woman, guns pointed at each other; Zane on the ground, looking so pale; Coach roaring away to protect her. And she thought of her mother and this morning and the doll. She thought of her house with a piercing yearning; she wanted to go home to her own bed, pull the covers over her head and sleep until she felt normal.

But the single thread running under all of that was *let him live, let him live, let him live.*

Finally, a portly guard with thinning blond hair came to the door. "You're free," he said, not unkindly. He pushed the buttons on the heavy gate and it swung open noiselessly. "There's a man waiting for you."

Her heart swelled with hope, and she rushed past them, thinking only of Zane, that he had not been as badly hurt as it appeared.

But of course it was not Zane, it was his friend Max who stood beyond the desk, his dark eyes very grave. Claire rounded the counter and went to him, but finding she couldn't voice anything, she only stared up at him. If someone asked her to choose Zane's associate from a crowd, this man would likely have been very far down her list. There was an old-world, almost princely attitude in his bearing, in the cut of his camel-hair coat and the barbering that left his dark hair rather rakishly long but exquisitely groomed. The Zane she'd known was a western man, wryly funny and very American.

But she remembered how he'd looked last night— had that only been last night?—in his Italian suit, his hair smoothed back from his face, and she realized with a tiny shock that he was just as comfortable in that world as he had been in hers.

"He is in surgery," he said. "Would you like to go to the hospital?"

"Yes." She stuck her hands in her pockets. "And my dog? Is he okay?"

He lifted a bandaged hand and wrist. "Better than I." A faint smile crossed the handsome face. "Very brave, your dog."

"I'm sorry…he was just protecting me."

He shook his head. "Do not apologize. I took him to my apartment. My housekeeper will see to his comfort." He took her elbow and directed her outside. The car was a midnight blue Mercedes, gleaming and new, which somehow did not surprise her. She settled, uncomfortably, and fastened her seat belt, and when he climbed in beside her, she smelled cologne she knew to cost upwards of one hundred dollars a bottle. When he started the car, she saw that he wore a simple ring, an enormous cabochon ruby set in gold. "Is that a Burma ruby?" she asked.

In some surprise, he smiled. "Very good. Are you fond of gems?"

"Not really. But Burmas are particularly beautiful." And wildly expensive. Claire couldn't even begin to estimate what it would have cost, and he wore it casually. For a moment, she said nothing, feeling acutely out of her class as he smoothly turned into traffic. He was the kind of person that made her most aware of her background, and she was always convinced that old money knew instantly she was from the wrong side of the tracks.

Let him live, let him live, let him live.

The chant ran under everything, coiling around her heart like a boa constrictor. She sucked in a breath against the sensation of panic and said the first thing that came to her head. "What are you, a duke or something?"

The instant the words were out of her mouth, she felt like an idiot. "I'm sorry. That was rude." She put her face in her hands. "I just can't seem to get a hold of myself."

"Quite understandable. You've had a very difficult few days, ending with a violent encounter and an arrest." He patted his pocket. "I have a clean handkerchief should you find you require it."

Claire hovered at the edge of a breakdown for one moment, but suddenly she found herself laughing instead. "The mark of a gentleman!" she said.

He chuckled. "Indeed."

"What happened to the Ghost?" she asked, suddenly remembering the pool of blood.

"You know her name." He gave her a hard look. "What else?"

She shrugged. "Most of it, I guess. I don't know who you work for, but I pieced the rest of it together. She's an assassin."

"Was. She's now quite dead, thanks in part to the heroics of your dog." He turned into the hospital parking lot and into a spot not far from the doors.

"And Zane? How bad is it?"

He paused a half beat before saying carefully, "I don't know."

Which told Claire all she needed to know. Bad. It was very bad.

Let him live, let him live, let him live.

It was several hours before the surgery was complete. Claire paced and drank bad coffee and wished for a shower. Finally a woman in blue scrubs emerged to tell them that Zane was going to be all right, and for whatever reason, that was the final straw. Claire collapsed into a trembling, exhausted heap. Max let her peek in at the sleeping Zane, surrounded by beeping machines, then took her to his elegantly appointed apartment and put her to bed.

In the morning, he fed her croissants and orange juice and drove her to the hospital before she had a chance to ask.

She expected to find him in intensive care, but they were directed to another, less critical area—though it was a private room. Windows showed a view of the bluffs surrounding the city, dusted with a sprinkling of snow, and the sight made Claire deeply hungry to go home. She just wanted this all to be over.

Zane lay in his bed, his black hair tousled and scattered over the white pillow, and the darkness made him seem pale. Yet he managed to look hearty and, in spite of the bandages and IV drips and pallid patterned blankets, as rugged as a mountain.

And suddenly she realized she had no idea what status they would have on this morning after. Her heart leapt as he stirred and opened his eyes, and when he saw Claire, she did not mistake the pleasure in his expression. "Hi," he said.

She took his hand. "Hi. How are you feeling?"

"Been better, but they tell me I'll live." He squeezed her hand. "I'm glad you're safe. Scared the hell out of me when I saw her coming up behind you." His jaw went tight. "How's Coach?"

"Fine." She glanced at Max. "Spoiled rotten by eating pâté, I'm afraid, but otherwise fine."

A faint smile touched his mouth, and he shifted to include Max. "Thanks, man."

"No problem."

"I saw the boss this morning," he said.

Max glanced at Claire, and she made a move to step back. "I'll let you two talk."

Zane tightened his grip. "Not yet."

Pleased, aching a little, she put her other hand over his. "Okay."

Zane glanced at Max, and the other man excused himself. As he left, Claire touched Zane's face. "I was so afraid."

"Claire," he said, and there was a heaviness to the way he said her name that evaporated her happiness like an iron on a damp collar. "Listen to me."

She started to shake her head, sensing what he was about to do, and feeling in her gut that it was wrong. He tightened his grip on her hand and pulled it to his mouth. "You're a hell of a woman. I couldn't have done this without you. There's a check coming to you, that should more than cover any expenses, but if it's short—"

Claire yanked her hand from his grip. "Don't." She backed away. "How dare you let me come in here, worried sick and half-insane with loving you, just to give me this little speech?" She shook her head. "You think you can walk away? Go ahead and try."

"Claire."

She moved to the door, ignoring him.

"Claire! Damn it! Stop for a minute."

She turned, lifting her chin. "I'm stopped."

"Please, come back over here." The genuine anguish laced through his need for control moved her. She sighed and stepped back to stand by the bed.

"Give me your hand."

She stuck it out, limply. He took it, kissed it again, pressed it along his face. "I told you. I kept telling you that you shouldn't make me out to be anything but what I am. I don't have a damned thing to give you, and you deserve somebody who can—"

"This is exactly what I don't want to hear," she said fiercely. "Some noble parting speech that's supposed to make me feel better about falling in love and making love with somebody I knew better than to get involved with. Just let me have my dignity, all right? I'm a big girl. I can handle it."

"You aren't listening." His jaw was tight, and his green eyes had never been more beautiful, more filled with emotion or light. "It wasn't play for me. I won't forget you."

She swallowed and shook her head, but couldn't find any way to block his need to speak. She bowed her head and rubbed her thumb against the length of his ring finger, memorizing the look of the lean beauty there.

"If I didn't care about you, I'd be selfish and tell you to come to Paris for a while, and spend more time with me. I'd tell you to forget about that little inn and your life, and come live mine.

"But for once in my life, maybe I can do the really right thing, and tell you to go home and find a man who can give you what you deserve—babies and steadiness and reliability."

She lifted her head and looked at him for a long moment, remembering the boyishness of his play on Christmas morning and the sound of his singing in church and the look of red, green and white icing on his hands. She took in the fine beauty of his face and the haunted look in his eye, and heard her mother's voice say, "Lord have mercy."

But she knew her mother was wrong this time. Larissa would have found his steady, upright honor a bore. She would have died rather than be dragged into a

church, and would have kicked out any man who suggested there might be something to it.

He'd given her Christmas, to make up for those
she'd lost, and she was touched by that. He'd given
her passion, and she felt fulfilled.

But beyond all that, he'd given her something she
had never even realized she needed—her own judg-
ment. She had not been wrong to love him, even if he
found he couldn't stay.

Claire bent over and kissed him. "Thank you for
everything," she said. "Goodbye."

Max accompanied her home, driving her and Coach
in Claire's slightly battered sports utility vehicle. He
lifted a brow at the sight of it, but by the time he'd
driven it a few miles, was enjoying it tremendously.
She discovered that she liked his wry, intelligent manner, and was glad Zane had a man of such steadiness
to call a friend.

He answered her rude question of the day before
with a wealth of stories revolving around the exploits
of a child born to an obscenely wealthy family in a
small European nation. Minor royalty, he said dismis-
sively, and she laughed.

As they drove up the rutted, winding, tiny road toward the Sea Breeze, however, Claire grew silent, only
now becoming aware of how much her life had
changed in the week since she'd roared down this road
in a snowstorm. Behind her, in the back seat, Coach
whined slightly, perhaps scenting his own neighborhood.

"I know just how you feel," she said to him.

And then they were turning up the driveway, and
there was her beautiful, graceful, well-tended home,

looking welcoming and cheerful. She wanted to whine herself at the peace of it, the porch stretching around the front, rocking chairs strategically placed to observe the best views, the beauty of the wide windows, the graceful protection of the towering monkey tree to one side. All of it. Hers.

Home.

Before the vehicle was fully stopped, she was out and running for the door, kicking aside the pile of accumulated mail, rushing in to—

Stand there. Smell it—pine and spice and her favorite potpourris. The rooms were cold, and she worried that the plants had suffered, but when she rushed into the dining room to check them, she saw that the impatiens were in full, glorious bloom, and even the enormous Swedish ivy that was prone to colds and droops of all sorts looked as perky as it had a week ago.

The Christmas tree had not fared quite so well, but even the sight of it, drooping and withered, failed to puncture her mood. "Poor thing," she said, and brushed a hand over a branch. Needles rained down to the carpet, and she grinned. "I'll do better next year."

"This is lovely, Claire," Max said behind her. "You have every right to be proud."

"Oh, I'm sorry I just rushed in here! Let me make some coffee and get you some dinner."

He smiled regretfully. "Alas, I must not leave our friend alone. You said there is a cab that will return me to the ferry?"

"Yes." She glanced at the clock. "If you hurry you can catch the next one out."

And finally, she was alone, for the first time in ages. Alone to putter in the kitchen and shiver there from

the holes in the windows, and make a pot of Sumerian
coffee, all for herself. Alone to take a batch of frozen
homemade soup from the freezer and heat it, slowly,
letting the scent fill her and the house with homey release, while she taped plastic over the broken panes in
the windows. Tomorrow, she'd call to have them properly replaced, and maybe while she was at it, have
someone haul away the Christmas tree. It was too big
for her, and she needed help with it.

She sorted the mail while she ate, and checked her
phone messages, then finally went upstairs, her sanctuary, to run a bath. Stripping naked with a sense of
wicked freedom, she padded between the graceful, sky-
lit bathroom and her room, selecting a warm flannel
nightgown to wear.

The books nearly unnerved her. Staring at a pile of
paperbacks she'd checked out from the library, Claire
was stabbed over and over with tiny little knives of
awareness she was not ready to face. She liked espionage thrillers as a rule, but that was out tonight. Ditto
the reincarnation romance. The mystery with a Native
American hero.

Feeling winded, she sank down on the bed and stared
at them, fighting panic that welled in her chest. She
had to have something to read. Something that would
carry her away, build a wall between herself and the
things she would have to face tomorrow morning.

Tossed casually on top of the bookcase was a ghost
story a guest had left behind. Yes! She snatched it joy-
fully from the case and carried it into the bathtub with
her. Drinking herb tea with chamomile to make her
sleep, she read until the water grew cold, then stumbled
to bed, numbed by heat and herbs and very real exhaustion. Coach padded into the room and slumped on

the floor beside the bed with a woofing sigh of relief. Draping her hand over the side of the bed, Claire rubbed his velvety ear and fell into a deep, dreamless sleep.

Zane stared out the window at a sky salted with stars. It was hospital quiet, which meant not very quiet at all. Contraptions on wheels clattered down the hall; nurses murmured in the room next door; machines whooshed; even the IV drip running into his arm had a blinking red light that beeped every so often.

If he hadn't felt like roadkill, it would have been more annoying. As it was, the painkillers they'd given him disconnected him from his body, though a stab of something made it through the haze every so often, sometimes a ping from the left half of his ribs, a low roar from his shoulder that buzzed behind everything, and the twinges of his reinjured knee.

From where he lay, he could see the edge of the Sound, stretching toward the islands between high bluffs. He wondered if Claire was home. What she was doing.

How long he would miss her like this. Over and over, he saw her big blue eyes shining at him before she kissed him goodbye this afternoon. A gentle kiss. A promise.

On one bluff nearby, an enormous house was outfitted with discreet lines of blue-and-white lights. They glowed into the night like hope, and he thought of the night he and Claire had spent in her truck, a night he'd spent staring at Christmas lights.

It was still Christmas right now. The thought bolted through him with an edge of surprise. He turned on his side, moving very carefully, and reached for the phone.

The effort left him breathing hard and he lay back, holding the headset against his stomach while he caught his breath. He closed his eyes and floated dizzily into a kaleidoscopic, slightly disturbing whirl of images. All of them Claire.

Blinking, he picked up the receiver and punched in numbers. A cheery voice on the other end of the line said, "Merry Christmas!"

"Same to you, Ma," he said.

"Zane! I've been hoping you'd get a chance to call. I missed you all day."

"Did you set a plate for me?"

"Always, son. Always. What have you done with your day?"

He hesitated. In the background, he could hear the voices of several women, and the sudden, booming laugh of an older man. "Am I keeping you from something, Ma? I just called to chat."

She chuckled. "I've been running for the phone every time it rang all day. You don't sound very good, honey. What's the problem?"

Zane opened his mouth, then closed it. In a rush he said, "Guess I'm getting a little too old to be playing this game." She assumed he was an adventurer of some kind—had no idea what he really did for a living. "I got kinda banged up and I'm lying here in a hospital bed, feeling sorry for myself."

"Oh, no." Her voice told him she bought the lightness of his comment. "What happened this time?"

All day, he'd felt a weight, or pressure, or something odd on his chest. He couldn't stop thinking of the small figure of the woman he'd killed, her very young face. What had driven her to make the kind of choices that would lead to a death on the street, far from home, on

Christmas Day? And as his mother waited for his response, he realized it could have gone either way. Him dead of a gunshot wound on a street in a strange city, on Christmas Day.

"Zane?"

"It's nothing, Ma. I'll be up and around in no time."

"I don't suppose you'd let me fly out to wherever you are and visit for a while."

If he said no, he knew he would not be able to resist calling Claire, asking her to keep him company while he spent yet another week in a cold, impersonal environment. And the one thing he was determined to do was leave her in peace. She deserved so much more.

"Well, I'll tell ya, I'm pretty beat this time. I wouldn't want you moaning and groaning about how I need to take care of myself."

"You know better. I can't help it."

"Can you limit it to five minutes, morning and evening?"

"Probably." She paused. "How far away are you?"

"It's not a bad trip. Couple hours." He gave her directions, room number, telephone number. "I can't get to my accounts at the moment, but I'll pay for the ticket when you get here, and I'll have a friend set up a room for you."

"Don't you worry about a thing, son. I can take care of myself." Then she asked, as if she wanted to stop herself and couldn't, "Did you go to church for Christmas?"

He couldn't say why it meant so much to him to say, "Yeah, Ma. I sure did."

Chapter 15

Claire believed in the catharsis of hard work. As a child, she had learned that spending her energy tidying things up was a far cry better than sitting around brooding about how unfair her life was. Before the interlude with Zane had turned her life—and heart—upside down, she had planned to spend the holidays giving the inn a thorough cleaning.

And for the next few days, she threw herself into the task. She arranged for the windows in the kitchen to be replaced and the holes in the plaster wall to be fixed, carefully avoiding the questioning glances of the repairman. She called in the carpet cleaners to scrub the main rooms downstairs, and while they were at work, the noise a comforting roar in the background, she took everything off the kitchen shelves, scrubbed them down and replaced the shelf paper. That gave her the idea of replacing the scented paper in the linen closet with a fresh batch, which required a day-long trip into town to Crabtree & Evelyn, the only place that carried the sort she liked. It cost a fortune, but Claire couldn't seem to care. The check from the agency came in the mail before the year turned—and even figuring interest or missing an entire week of guests at the inn, Claire couldn't imagine how she'd earned quite that much money.

But there was no way to complain, and she deposited the sum in her bank, thinking it might buy the new sofa arrangement she'd been eyeing for the living room.

Throughout the cleaning frenzy, she managed to avoid the room where Zane had briefly slept, leaving it until she felt a little stronger. Each day, she put it on the list of things to do, and each evening, she had to transfer it to the next day's list of chores.

But at the end of the week, she had a flurry of phone reservations, musicians mostly, coming to the island for an impromptu gathering of school chums. They fit nicely before the bookings she had for later in the month. By the tone of their calls, she gathered it would be an exuberant, unconventional group. They also had an array of interesting food requests—one diabetic, two vegetarians and one allergic to chemical food additives. She billed herself as catering to special diets, so she was not unprepared, but it took careful planning to meet the needs of such a variety all at once. They would arrive in three days—she had an enormous amount of shopping and planning to do.

Just what the doctor ordered. Happily humming to herself, she laid in a huge supply of organic fresh fruits and vegetables and meats, looked up recipes for the various special needs, baked and froze a variety of bread doughs, and fell into bed every night with healthy exhaustion.

The morning before they arrived, she could no longer avoid cleaning Zane's room. There was a young mother from town who helped clean the rooms when Claire had a full house, but she would not arrive until the following morning. Claire knew this job was one she had to do herself.

The morning of the fifth dawned like a January jewel—the sky a dazzling shade of turquoise that formed a breathtaking backdrop for the greens of birch and Douglas fir. Sunlight, bright yellow, poured through the sparkling clean windows, falling over the plants and floors and clean carpets like a glaze of butter. With pride, Claire walked through the rooms to make sure everything was ready, adjusting a chair here, a plant stand there, and then—armed with vacuum cleaner, fresh sheets and feather duster—she marched down the hall to one of her very best rooms, and flung open the door.

The remembrance of starry nights slammed her so hard she found herself taking a step backward. And she was not prepared to find so much evidence of his visit still lingering, unchanged. Coach, busy till that moment, came running from his post by the dining room windows, a soft, welcoming whine in his throat.

"It's not him," she said. "Just his stuff."

Coach pushed by her, his nose to the floor as he traced the invisible trail of feet over the carpet, to the bed, into the bathroom. Claire simply stood there, staring at the rumpled bed, the towels flung over the back of a chair, and wondered why she hadn't realized it would be like this. Had she expected little elves to come in and do the cleaning for her?

Coach came out of the bathroom and leaned heavily against the bed, the way he leaned against her knees when he wanted her approval, and turned his nose upward, to where Zane had slept, lifting his head as if he could see the man. It pierced her. For a long, roaring moment, she let everything rush back through her—his arrival and their journey, the sound of his laughter and the slight tilt of his green eyes, the sweet presents he'd given her on Christmas morning, and the sound of his singing. The images ripped through her, agonizing and unbearably dear, and abashed, she followed her dog's lead. She walked over to the bed, picked up the pillow and held it to her face, breathing in that scent.

It made her dizzy, and brought back sensory images of his hair on her face, his mouth on her neck, the sound of his satisfaction rolling from his throat. "Oh, Zane," she said aloud. "We miss you so much. Please come home."

For a moment, she allowed herself the comfort of holding that pillow to her chest, then she swallowed, took a deep breath and put it aside. "Sorry, honey," she said to Coach, "I have to clean up." Firmly, she reached for the blankets and stripped the bed.

In an hour it was ready for the next guest, but Claire carried the pillow with Zane's scent on it and put it upstairs. She could allow herself that much nostalgia. When she put it on the bed, Coach promptly leapt up, curled into a ball and covered it with his body. "You have to stop," she said sadly. "He's gone."

Coach licked her wrist but did not move. And although she knew the warm, hairy scent of clean dog would eradicate the lingering scent of the man who had slept there, she didn't have the heart to take the pillow away.

* * *

By evening, Claire had a full house of middle-aged musicians—a group as eccentric as any she'd ever had. They carried in flutes and horns and even drums, and spent the evening drinking wine with other friends who came in from another hotel, and gobbling down snacks as quickly as Claire could put them out. They wandered between rooms and spilled out to the porch, laughing, tapping out rhythms, singing, even dancing when a flutist and violinist sailed into a snappy Celtic piece.

It was exuberant. It was glorious. Claire was also going to make a fortune—and she was so busy she made a mental note to call in some of her part-time workers for the rest of the stay. She'd had a couple scheduled to come in, here and there, during the busiest times, but suspected she was going to need at least one other set of hands round the clock throughout this visit. On the third floor, she kept a couple of rooms for that purpose—pleasant, plain rooms she'd furnished with white wicker, fancying someday they'd be rooms for her children.

When the group tired, Claire cleaned up quickly, set the coffeemaker to start at 5:00 a.m. and flopped on her bed to get as much rest as she could before it all started over again. Her tired bones sang with the pleasure of honest exertion, and she drifted off peacefully, thinking that she was blessed indeed, to have found her place in life.

The musicians ploughed through the breakfast buffet like a cloud of locusts and rushed off to some morning event, leaving Claire and the two women she'd hired to clean the rooms and prepare the evening meal at their leisure. "Quite a group!" commented Mary Ivers, a young mother who liked the job because she could bring her ten-month-old son. In his playpen in a safe corner of the kitchen, he chewed on a biscuit, making noises of pleasure to Coach, who sat alongside the baby, alert for any dropped tidbit.

"They're a lot of fun." Claire mixed whole grain flours with baking powder and salt, and made a hole in the pile for the liquid ingredients. Next to her, Mary scrubbed and grated carrots for the cake she was making in honor of Epiphany, the twelfth day of Christmas.

Both of them heard the sound at the same moment. "What is that?" Mary asked.

Claire grinned. "Drums? Our musicians must have decided to change location." Wiping her hands, she bent down and grabbed the baby. "Let's go see."

Coach, spying a particularly wide spray of crumbs the baby had dropped on the floor, stayed to slurp it up. Bouncing the baby on her hip in time to the music, Claire opened the front door and halted in delight. The musicians had indeed returned—and brought hordes of their friends. The drummers were marching up the driveway, tapping with sticks on snares or pounding with hands on congas, and the sound lifted into the bright morning like a celebration.

"One, two three…" Mary counted. "There's twelve! Twelve drummers drumming."

Claire laughed and called out, "Bravo!"

But they weren't finished with their impromptu display. Claire and Mary stepped onto the porch to watch the show, the drummers lined up side by side, looking at one another, counting off the time. Behind them a clutter of flutists and violinists and even a guitarist made their instruments ready. Some Claire recognized, some she did not. All were obviously part of the same group—she thought idly that they must have filled every room on the island.

"What are they doing?" Mary whispered.

"I don't know. Maybe there will be some lords a-leaping or something." She chuckled.

A hush fell over them, and Claire felt a shiver of anticipation rush up her spine.

And then they began to play. Her very favorite Christmas carol, the one she could never hear without getting choked up, the one she identified with most strongly. The drums began...pah-rum pah-pum pum, rum-pah pum pum, and then the flutes joined in, and the violins, taking up the bittersweet melody.

Claire made a sound, and tried to catch it back with her fingers, fingers she discovered were trembling. Her heart suddenly pounded louder than the drums.

And from behind her came a wild, mournful howl, a cry of greeting and loss and joy that only a dog could make, and before Claire could fully register the sound, Coach flung himself at the screen door and streaked between Mary and Claire with enough force to knock them sideways. He didn't bark—he whined and howled as he ran, ducking between rows of musicians, leaving puffs of dirt in his wake.

Blindly, Claire turned and handed the baby to Mary, moving as if in a dream. She floated on the music that swelled up around her, floated down the steps and between drummers, who moved aside for her, smiling indulgently.

She stopped. Coach did not—he flung himself at the man at the end of the driveway with a kind of delirious glee, slamming into his knees, wiggling around to put his head against his legs and gaze up adoringly, whining, licking his lips, shifting again. Laughing, Zane bent, rubbing the dog vigorously with the arm that was free, bending his face close so Coach could lick it.

"I am a poor boy, too, pah-rum pah-pum pum…"

Claire closed her eyes, afraid to move, afraid it was a dream, then opened them again. Zane still stood there, dressed in a clean white shirt with a tie, and a pair of close-fitting jeans, his hair loose on his shoulders. He met her gaze, and she saw worry and uncertainty cross his face.

"You were right," he said simply.

And at last, Claire smiled. Then, like her dog, she leapt forward, her heart in her eyes where he could see it, tears of joy rushing down her face, not stopping until she had flung herself, her whole self, into the vise of his arms, hugging him so tightly that she couldn't breathe. "I knew you'd come."

Zane gripped her as close as he could, drinking in the smell of her hair and the sugar scent of her skin. His heart swelled a thousand times its normal size, and he couldn't breathe, so he lifted his head and kissed her. It made him so dizzy he swayed and he gripped her tighter. "I missed you like a limb," he said roughly.

Next to him came the sound of a throat being cleared discreetly, and Zane smiled, took a breath. Holding Claire's hand, he turned. "Ma, this is Claire Franklin. I think you two will like each other."

To his amazement, it was his mother who had tears in her green eyes. She moved forward, her gait only faintly uneven as she held out her arms to the small innkeeper. "I've always wanted a daughter," she said.

Claire smiled, her face radiant, and embraced her. "And I always wanted a mother," she whispered.

The musicians cheered and started breaking up, playing silly pieces, romantic little swirls, as Claire took both Zane and his mother's hands. "I have a lot of work to do. Please come in and let me make you comfortable."

"Actually, if you'll point me in the right direction," Mrs. Hunter said, "I'd like to powder my nose."

"Of course." Claire waved to a woman on the porch. "Go see Mary. She'll help you."

The musicians were scattering, too, and Zane was grateful. "Wait," he said, catching her hand. "I just need two minutes."

She looked up, her eyes steady and calm and strong. There was no hint of the vulnerable little girl he'd glimpsed during Christmas. She touched his face with wonder. "I feel like I'm going to wake up from a dream. I'm so glad you're here."

"Are you, Claire?" He was botching it. He felt tangled up with nerves, with anticipation, with fear. It had seemed so obvious in the hotel room. After nearly a week of misery, he'd awakened yesterday morning feeling as clear as he had about anything.

But now he was afraid. He closed his eyes, took a breath.

"What is it, Zane?"

He swallowed, opened his eyes and pulled something out of his pocket. "I quit the Organization," he said. "It'll be a while before I'm up to speed, but when I get the details worked out, I'll be sending my résumé out to the police department. Maybe, uh, I can train a hound." He looked at Coach. "No offense." The dog licked his hand.

"It's a wonderful idea." Now she looked a little unsure. "There will certainly be plenty of work."

"Uh, the other thing is…" He felt heat in his ears and took the box from his pocket. With fingers made a little thick and clumsy with nerves, he opened it and said in a rush, "I'm in love with you, Claire. I know it was fast, and maybe you need some time, but I've been waiting all my life for you, for what we had." He stared at the ring, a sapphire with a star breaking the light in shimmering waves. It had made him think of her eyes, when they were full of mischief. "Take all the time you need, but I wanted you to know my intentions are honorable. That I don't just want to come and shack up with you. I want to marry you. If and when you think it's right."

And finally, there were the tears he had somehow wanted, the tears that let him know she was overcome…and her smile said they were tears of joy. "Now," she said clearly.

"Oh, that was the right answer," he said, and bent down to sweep her up, sweep her close, seeing a score of peaceful, Claire-filled years ahead.

"I love you, Zane," she whispered, and kissed his ear, her arms fierce and faithful around him, making him whole.

Epilogue

She crept out of her room and down the stairs, silent as a mouse that didn't stir on Christmas Eve. Her slippers made no sound on the stairs. When she reached the bottom, she crept along the edge of the wall, giddiness welling up in her chest so that she had to stop and cover her mouth to keep back the laughter. Her kindergarten teacher said she laughed too much, anyway, but Noelle thought she must have got it from her mommy and daddy because they laughed even more than she did.

This was her favorite part of her birthday, coming down the stairs late on Christmas night after everyone thought she was asleep. Her grandma was sleeping in the best guest room, since they didn't have any guests during Christmas week at all. Mommy said it was family time. Noelle's brother, only two, was asleep, too, but she figured he'd like this, too, when he got a little older.

She heard the voices before she got to the door. The rumbling laughter of her daddy, the whisper and giggle of her mommy. With a dash, she crossed the bar of light and danced into the darkness of the dining room, where the tree sparkled still in red and blue and green and white, all glittery and tall. Everyone said her mommy had the prettiest tree on the island, and Noelle would definitely agree.

She bumped into the soft, fleshy foot of a person, and had to cover her mouth to keep back a screech. "Grandma!" she whispered. "What are you doing here?"

Warm arms scooped her up, plopped her down on the soft leg, not the hard one, though Noelle didn't mind either one. Grandma let her look at the fake leg sometimes, and it was very cool the way the knee worked. "What are you doing here?" her grandma asked.

Noelle turned and pointed silently. Across the hall, in a candlelit room, were her mommy and daddy, sitting in front of a fire. Her daddy's braid came all the way to the middle of his back. He sat behind Mommy, his arms around her shoulders, his chin on her hair, and Mommy leaned against him, her legs stretched out in front of her. It was what they did every Christmas night. Built a fire and sat together, close and quiet, and Noelle just liked the feeling of love it gave her. She knew, if she wandered in there, that they'd make room for her. They'd put their arms around her and hold her and kiss her.

But on Christmas night, she just liked to see them for a minute. The best part of Christmas was this minute.

"Pretty special, isn't it?" Grandma said.

"Yes," Noelle answered, and sighed happily as her mommy turned her head and kissed her daddy, right on the lips. "The best."

* * * * *

SILHOUETTE
SENSATION®

AVAILABLE FROM 24TH DECEMBER 1999

THE TOUGH GUY AND THE TODDLER
Diane Pershing

Within weeks Jordan Carlisle had aided in the rescue of a kidnapped child, begun a flirtation with intensely sexy detective Dominic D'Annunzio…and learned that her own son might be alive. If they found her toddler, would her tough guy stay?

LIKE FATHER, LIKE DAUGHTER
Margaret Watson

Not a night passed that Becca Johnson didn't dream about one long-ago summer and a certain handsome wanderer. Now, finally, he'd come home, but things were different. She was a confident alluring woman with a child to protect—a child with his blue eyes!

THE MIRACLE MAN Sharon Sala

Heartbreaker

Antonette Hatfield wanted a baby, but Mr Right had never come along. Then US Marshal Lane Monday was washed ashore—the answer to her every prayer… But Lane didn't want to get involved—pleasure without price wasn't his style…

ONCE MORE A FAMILY Paula Detmer Riggs

Grady Hardin made it his mission to reunite his family—he was determined to bring back his abducted son and reawaken the love of the only woman he'd ever wanted. But he'd forgotten the intense passion and deep emotions his ex-wife Ria had always aroused in him…

9912

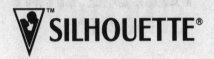

FOLLOW THAT BABY

Everybody's looking for a missing pregnant woman in the exciting new cross-line mini-series from Silhouette®.

FREE
2 BOOKS
AND A SURPRISE GIFT!

We would like to take this opportunity to thank you for reading this Silhouette® book by offering you the chance to take TWO more specially selected titles from the Sensation™ series absolutely FREE! We're also making this offer to introduce you to the benefits of the Reader Service™ —

★ FREE home delivery
★ FREE monthly Newsletter
★ FREE gifts and competitions
★ Exclusive Reader Service discounts
★ Books available before they're in the shops

Accepting these FREE books and gift places you under no obligation to buy; you may cancel at any time, even after receiving your free shipment. Simply complete your details below and return the entire page to the address below. **You don't even need a stamp!**

YES! Please send me 2 free Sensation books and a surprise gift. I understand that unless you hear from me, I will receive 4 superb new titles every month for just £2.70 each, postage and packing free. I am under no obligation to purchase any books and may cancel my subscription at any time. The free books and gift will be mine to keep in any case.

S9EC

Ms/Mrs/Miss/Mr ....Initials...................................
BLOCK CAPITALS PLEASE

Surname...

Address...

....

....Postcode ....

Send this whole page to:
UK: FREEPOST CN81, Croydon, CR9 3WZ
EIRE: PO Box 4546, Kilcock, County Kildare (stamp required)